I0824052

SEARCHING FOR FIRE

J. SPEER

WORKBOOK PRESS LLC
187 E Warm Springs Rd,
Suite B285 Las Vegas NV 89119 USA

Website: https://workbookpress.com/
Hotline: 1-888-818-4856
Email: admin@workbookpress.com

Ordering Information:
Quantity sales. Special discounts are available on quantity purchases by corporations, associations, and others. For details, contact the publisher at the address above.

ISBN-13: 978-1-963718-47-8 Paperback Version
978-1-963718-48-5 Digital Version

REV. DATE: 02/24/2024

TABLE OF CONTENTS

Chapter 1 : A Deceitful Pact.............................1

Chapter 2 : A Meeting of Minds.............................9

Chapter 3 : A Narrow Escape.............................15

Chapter 4 : An Angry Warrior.............................27

Chapter 5 : Snake Charmer.............................30

Chapter 6 : At the Water's Edge.............................39

Chapter7 : Making an Ally.............................48

Chapter 8 : The Story of Sam.............................55

Chapter 9 : An Unlikely Guardian.............................58

Chapter 10 : Dream of Fire.............................61

Chapter 11 : The Tracker.............................64

Chapter 12 : A Shocking Discovery.............................66

Chapter 13 : Don't Stay at the Inn.............................76

Chapter 14 : On the Outskirts of Silver Springs.............................89

Chapter 15 : Closer.............................93

Chapter 16 : A Tragic Backstory.............................94

Chapter 17 : Beware of the Forest.............................96

Chapter 18 : Unexpected Visitors.............................106

Chapter 19 : One Thousand-Plus Feet Underground.............................110

Chapter20 : Bat Attack.............................115

Chapter21 : The Deepest Pit.............................119

Chapter22 : Battle of the Beasts.............................125

Chapter23 : Earth, Wind, and Fire.............................131

"Great first work! Several images are haunting along the heroes' journey. A real page turner at times. Such a creative introduction to an intriguing fantasy world." ***(Amazon Review)***

"A compelling, involving tale that excels in revealing the growth of all characters as they confront higher purposes and challenges than their individual daily lives." ***(Midwest Book Review)***

"An epic tale that shines a great light on indigenous spiritualism and mythology. The world and plot kept me highly engrossed and I was continually impressed with the grand scope of the story." ***(Goodreads Review)***

"It's a good story to say the least...pretty impressive for the first book. I would not mind reading a sequel if one is ever made." ***(Goodreads review)***

Searching for Fire

J. Speer

Prologue: A Clash of Spirits

This is not our first world.

In the beginning, the Sun Spirit created our land and established the Elemental Code for our existence. All the living creatures inhabited this world for the benefit of the Great Spirits in the sky. When the hearts of the land's inhabitants decayed, these same Great Spirits rained fire down from the sky.

Among the smoke and ash, a second world was reborn. It prospered, but as with the cycle of the first, the decay returned. The Great Spirits chose this time to bury our world in ice.

As to the third world, our people were gifted with the presence of the fire bringer named Ahiga. One day, the Great Fire Spirit, a divine immortal, noticed a beautiful Indian woman. He hid among the rocks watching the maiden gather water for her family at the spring. Every day he watched the girl visit the spring. Eventually, he appeared to her. Over time, the two friends fell in love. The young maiden trusted him so much so that when the Great Fire Spirit revealed his true nature, she was not frightened by his divine appearance.

Time passed. In the form of a man, Ahiga, the Great Fire Spirit, eventually presented himself to her people. He appeared as a stranger and returned many days, again and again, until finally he asked for the hand of the Indian maiden. In exchange, he shared with our people the secret of his fire craft. His fire could be used for so many tasks.

The days progressed, and time passed happily. Eventually, the maiden was laden with child, both human and immortal.

Meanwhile, the Storm Spirit named Haseya, the strongest

spirt of all, was making plans to destroy and rebuild from the third world. The Great Fire Spirit Ahiga, who had returned to the heavens for diplomacy, sent word of this through the messenger of a tiny black spider. The spider descended from the sky on one small silver thread.

The tiny black spider worked day and night for many moons, weaving a giant silver silken bridge of webs across the great waters so our people could escape the Storm Spirit's destruction. The clouds overhead grew dark, and thunder and lightning struck the land. The inhabitants of this world knew what would come and shook with fear.

Meanwhile, the tiny spider spirit led the pregnant woman and her family across the bridge. The waves crashed, and the wind howled. The storm threatened to break the threads, but it held secure for the people and for those few creatures brave and wise enough to follow. The Storm Spirit discovered the bridge. In that moment, enraged by this defiance, the Storm Spirit goddess Haseya attempted to undue the bridge with thunderous waves. The waters churned with magnificent power. The waters frothed and the wind howled. Although he was not as strong as the Storm Spirit, the Fire Spirit rose up against the waves and used great fire to push them back.

For this disobedience, the violent Storm Spirit Haseya sent sharp thunderbolts into the web of the bridge. Many of those animals and humans crossing became entangled and entrapped. Others eventually fell, tumbling into the dark waters below as the bridge broke apart and disappeared into the deadly waves.

The pregnant woman and her family made it to safety, though. They lived through the rebirth of the world. It became the fourth world. The Great Spider Mother led her family, our ancestors, to safety among the mountain cliffs. And it was here, in this valley, that she taught our people how to build our homes within the mountainside and how to thrive as a community. Great Spider Mother taught us many things, and when her tasks to the Fire Spirit Ahiga were fulfilled, she left. Some say she passed on from this world. Some believe she will return to guide our people again. Some say Ahiga will return himself, but that will not happen until this world decays ...

Ahiga, the Fire Spirit, had broken the Elemental Code. As decreed by this Elemental Code of Spirits, the Great Fire Spirit, for his indiscretion, was chained and bound eternally with fireproof links in the darkest cavern of the deepest pit below the earth's crust. He could never see the Indian maiden again and never know his own son until the rebirth of a new world.

The woman gave birth. She lived and eventually died, passing on to the spirit realm.

There have been many centuries, many lives, and many generations since the creation of this world.

Our people are sworn to never leave this valley until the days when the Great Spider Mother will return. Prophecy says that those who venture out past the Snake River will be doomed to the great destruction of this world. Here in the safety of our valley and cliff dwellings, we live a simple existence in peace and harmony. Outside the world continues, but here we behave as the Great Spider Mother warned us. We do not want to provoke the Great Spirits into anger again, particularly the Storm Spirit Haseya.

Meanwhile, among the third-world animals that crossed the old spider bridge, there are some wicked and ancient creatures who should have been destroyed. They would do harm to our people if given the chance. They walk the olden ways, and they shape-shift through witchcraft. Their spirits are decayed to black.

They should never be trusted.

Chapter One: A Deceitful Pact

In the eaves of a tall green ponderosa pine, high above in the forest of Hanahu Valley in the canyon lands of the Southwest, there sat perched a young boy of nine years old. He had brown hair and light brown eyes. He played a little wooden flute. Along the length of his shoulder, a pet lizard named Izou ran. The boy had some talent at the flute, which had recently been given to him by his grandfather. The boy worked his fingers across the holes of the flute and pursed his lips to change the sound of the musical notes. Meanwhile, the pet lizard ran down his back familiarly. Then Izou ran along the length of the tree branch timber. They were interrupted by friends below, other young boys his age that came here to do races.

"Kokopelli!" they called to him up in the tree.

The boy put away the lizard and flute in his leather satchel. He swiftly and athletically descended the tree. There were jokes told among the boys and laughter. They played some, laughed and smiled, and raced back toward the cliff village. They raced ahead through cornfields and vegetable gardens, along a little stream, and to the base of the cliff. There, they began to ascend quickly ladder after ladder, farther and farther up and up and up into the hillside and cliffs toward their home above. They passed residences and stores where baskets were woven and rugs, pottery, jewelry, and clothing were made. There were places to barter here. Places for food, herbs, hunted meat, or procured fish—whatever someone might need. As they ran, the boy passed his mother working a floor loom, and she told him his father was looking for him. One by one, the boys said goodbye and stopped at their individual residences. Kokopelli was one of the last to leave, having ascended to a higher adobe cliff home. His friend Tetu waved one last time and turned the corner ahead as Kokopelli lifted the leather flap to his home. Little would they see each other in the days to come.

On the next day, Kokopelli's father and relatives took the boy on a hunt in the valley far away from the others. They searched for wild pigs or fowl and, as always, checked the traps. At one point in the hunt, Kokopelli saw something stirring the brush in the distance to his left. He heard a noise, and he separated from the hunting group to uncover the source of the disturbance. A silent dire wolf startled him. It was a wolf but much larger than a typical timber wolf and more menacing because it was a decayer wolf from the previous world. Kokopelli quickly turned away from it, running farther into the prairie grass and away from his group. Over his shoulder, he saw that now a pack of large wolves followed, chasing the boy purposefully into the tall prairie grasses out of the woods. Kokopelli abruptly fell over a small ledge into a ravine and was knocked out by the side of a hard rock on the dirt ground.

Other dire wolves were also near the ravine, as if waiting for the child to fall. They approached cautiously at first and then circled the boy's body several times. They nudged him. He did not move. One wolf stood over the child and began to bare his sharp teeth, threatening to sink them into the exposed flesh. From the tall prairie grass emerged a low, throaty growl, a warning to the wolf to back off. The prairie grass rustled and swayed, and then the alpha pushed through violently. He was a predatory Hyaenodon of old from the previous world, a decayer, nearly twice the size of the others, and he strongly cuffed the threatening wolf, tossing it sideways in the dirt. The Hyaenodon looked at the other wolves and bared his fangs, growling low and deep until the other wolves stood back, one by one, bowing down low to the earth.

"This is not the one. He's just a means to an end. We must wait," the Hyaenodon growled.

And with that, the Hyaenodon let out a loud, long howl to draw the hunters toward the body. The wolves darted into the tall prairie grass, moving quickly away in the direction far from the hunters. They retreated into the woods and watched the unfolding scene when the father and relatives found the boy. The father gently picked up his son, and they promptly headed back to the cliff village.

That night, in his adobe, Kokopelli was cared for by the village medicine man named Sani. The outlook was grave, a severe swelling in his head, and there was low talk outside the hut of his poor health situation. The mother watched the boy's breathing carefully. The medicine man worried if the boy's body might be broken, unable to heal. He stayed late into the night until he could do no more for the family. Sadly, he headed out into the darkness of the night. The father and mother took their sleeping mat and placed it close to the boy. The father soon fell asleep beside his son. The mother and the boy's younger sister talked for a little while. The mother tucked the daughter into her sleeping mat with her little kachina doll gripped close to her chest, and then the whole family drifted off to slumber. It was near to midnight when they finally rested.

Beyond the fields on a plateau, the Hyaenodon waited and watched the firelights extinguish in the cliff village. Alone in the dark, his eyes glowed yellow in the moonlight. He growled very low. He burst into a rapid sprint and propelled himself off the plateau far above the valley below into the starry night sky. In midair as he fell, he effortlessly shape-shifted into a black raven, swooping low and gracefully over the fields and stream. He landed and shifted abruptly again into a black bear, making a rapid and powerful gait. His name was Hashkeh Naabah, meaning angry warrior, and his abilities were eons upon eons old. As he reached obstacles in his path, he plowed ferociously through them. As he neared the village, he was more careful to be quiet and stealthy. On the outskirts of the village at the base of the cliff where the first ladder ascended, he cleverly shifted again into a black scorpion and moved discretely up the cliff, up and up, ladder upon ladder, past home after home until he reached the family's adobe hut. The scorpion entered the little room moving across the glowing embers of the remains of the fire. Amid the spiraling smoke, he shifted into a mountain lion spirit.

The big mountain lion purred, brushing softly along the length of the sleeping mother.

"Mistress, wake up," he whispered.

The spirit of the sleeping mother named Shoshanna rose from her body as well to converse with the mountain lion spirit.

"You know, your son will likely die tomorrow," said the mountain lion spirit. He was straightforward in his tone, neither aggressive nor pleasant. "I can help you," he said after a pause. He sat back on his haunches, took a claw, and lazily drew a symbol in the dirt.

"What do you want?" asked the distressed mother, looking at him. She hesitated.

"Just a trifling matter, nothing much really." He shrugged. He looked her directly in the eyes. His claw stopped tracing in the dirt, and he shifted his weight purposefully forward. "Do you want my help?"

Shoshanna looked at the mountain lion spirit. She looked down. "Yes," she murmured.

"Good," he replied and grinned, tilting his large cat head to the side. "Then consider it done." He looked down at his paw, retracted the claw, and began slowly cleaning his paw. "I will make good on the bargain at a later time perhaps. You've chosen well."

Shoshanna did not trust the mountain lion spirit. "Fix it," she said under her breath, and her spirit returned to her resting body. The mother briefly moaned. She shook her head in her sleep ever so slightly and then was still once more.

That night, as the others rested, the mountain lion spirit

moved close, very close to the boy. He shifted once more into a humanlike creature. He was pale and gaunt. He looked quite sickly. His hands were claws and his eyes like black voids. He incanted words from an ancient language. Using the symbol drawn into the dirt, he shifted some ash into the circle and then rapidly expelled it out of the circle. Speaking in tongue, he then covered the symbol with white sand. After completing the mysterious ritual, the creature swiftly cleaned up his work. He shifted again into a black scorpion, crawling up the side of the adobe hut and disappearing into the night through a crack in the wall over the door. Meanwhile, inside the hut, no one moved except for a barely discernible movement from the small kachina doll the young sister held in her sleep.

The boy healed. The next morning, he awoke to the great relief of all.

Nights later, the medicine man Sani was alone in his residence when he heard a knock on the left wall of the adobe. He looked promptly around to make certain he was alone. Then he moved a few baskets and rocks in the wall to reveal a hidden tunnel. This tunnel, however, was quite small, too small for humans. Standing in the tunnel was the little kachina doll, a magical guardian spirit.

"We must call the council," the doll named Yanaha said. "I waited until I could escape and come to you. Something terrible has happened. The boy didn't heal all by himself. He was healed by one of them—the decayed ones. I fear we are in grave trouble."

Sani and Yanaha spoke of the events that transpired a few nights before. He told Sani of the mountain lion spirit and the strange humanoid creature, of the incantation, and of the shape-shifting.

"This is not good; this is not good," said Yanaha.

"I know," Sani replied. "We knew this could happen at some point."

"The people are not ready for this."

"They will have to be. Call the council."

The medicine man Sani looked down and nodded. Later, he climbed to the council chamber of the cliff village. He put a sleeping enchantment upon the entire village and called together a meeting of the council, but not what one would normally expect. It was a council of the guardian kachina dolls.

Upon the birth of each baby girl in the village, a special kachina doll was bestowed on her by the medicine man Sani. Little did the girls know that these were crafted magical spirit guardians tasked with protecting the cliff dwellers. They lived in each adobe home as playmates for the girls and secretly kept watch over all activities for the medicine man.

The villagers slept, and so, one by one, the kachina dolls gathered from almost every home in the cliff dwellings. Each kachina doll was unique and wore a special costume of spectacular brilliant colors. They were bold and lively, as the medicine man took special care to craft each personality to fit the personalities of the children in the village. They were guardians to the children and their families and took their duties of protection very seriously. That night the council meeting was raucous and argumentative. There was much debate on what to do. Finally, it was decided that the medicine man should consult the leaders of the forest—the ancient creatures like himself. For the medicine man was ancient too. He was not just the medicine man Sani but secretly also the son of the Fire Spirit—part divine God, part human ... aging slowly in time. It was decided that the medicine man would go to the ancient ones. He would make the journey, and the kachina dolls would stay back to protect the village. He would find the ancient nature spirits who crossed his mother's spider bridge and make a pact for peace with the humans.

Sani left the village the next day, packing all he needed for the journey into the forest. He asked the kachina dolls to watch over his people. He brought his crow, the one that flew ahead and scouted for him and was a messenger to the ancient nature spirits he would encounter in the wilderness.

Many nights passed until he gathered with the nature spirits one evening as the glow of firelight bounced off the edges of a rock wall deep in the forest. These ancient nature spirits made it very clear that they would not be involved in human matters. However, they did not want the woman indebted to Hashkeh Naabah either. He was a shape-shifter, a crossover from the old ways. He practiced the blackest magic and alchemy. Although he shifted into many creatures, he was unable to shift into complete human form, and so in his true form, he appeared as a horrid creature, almost humanlike with talons for hands and eyes like black voids.

The ancient nature spirits made many guesses surmising as to what this decayer wanted. They created a new pact with Sani. If they were ever needed in battle against Hashkeh Naabeh, the kachina dolls could call and they would answer. That is all they were willing to give at this time. They concurred avidly that there was no need for unnecessary conflict at this time.

Half-heartedly, Sani returned to the village. The kachina dolls continued to watch over Kokopelli and his younger sister Mai as they grew older. They were both active and well-loved. Kokopelli became a great flute player, always willing to entertain his family and friends.

In a few years, Shoshanna, their mother, became pregnant with another child. Kokopelli and his sister would have another sibling. But Hashkeh Naabah returned again as a mountain lion spirit to the mother spirit in her sleep. He asked for the child.

"Just leave it in the woods," he said. "It will soon be forgotten."

The mother was repulsed by the idea and originally said no. The decayer warned that an accident could be arranged again for both her older children, Kokopelli and Mai, this time.

"They matter little to me. Perhaps one may disappear," he

said again, casually drawing a symbol in the dirt with his sharpened claw.

And so, the mother conceded.

But again, the kachina dolls were aware of this exchange. Word was passed to the medicine man. The time had come to talk to the boy Kokopelli.

Chapter Two: A Meeting of Minds

A few months after her second encounter with the mountain lion spirit, Kokopelli's mother, Shoshanna, gave birth to a beautiful baby boy she named Kai. Both mother and father were so proud of the new arrival as were many members of the cliff-dwelling community. There was a celebration in their honor put together by the medicine man of the village. The invited guests met in the council chamber adobe building. There was wonderful feasting and pleasantries. Music was played and many stories exchanged, and good times were had by all. The new baby, Kai, was presented to the community, and the mother, Shoshanna, smiled with a touch of sadness in her eyes but remained stoic throughout the event. The baby was swaddled in warm blankets made especially from her loom, and some villagers brought gifts for the family as well. Kokopelli and his younger sister Mai, who were fifteen and thirteen by now, also engaged in the festivities, and Kokopelli played his flute at times to the enjoyment of all. As it got later, one by one the guests departed the council chamber. Mother and Father and baby Kai returned to their adobe hut near the top of the cliffs. The medicine man had requested of them that Kokopelli and Mai stay behind to help with the cleanup, and both parents graciously consented. Soon, all the party goers had left the chamber except the three who were now alone.

"I'm glad we have some time alone to talk. Please sit. There are a few matters I would like to discuss with you," began the medicine man.

He motioned for Kokopelli and Mai to sit across from him in the council chamber. Together, the three sat cross-legged. Sani smiled at them, and they smiled back pleasantly.

Sani was not sure how to begin. He asked them, "How old do you suppose I am?"

They both looked at each other and smiled back. Kokopelli offered, "I would guess forty."

The medicine man nodded and looked at Mai, who also smiled and said, "Well, maybe forty-five."

Sani laughed a little to put them at ease and then said, "Would you be surprised to learn I am much older, in fact?" And they both laughed until he nodded again. "Yes, I am much older and have guarded this cliff village for a much longer time than you would expect."

Kokopelli's and Mai's eyes widened a little.

The medicine man sighed and said, "I am entrusting the two of you with a very important matter. I need your promise of secrecy."

The two teenagers nodded, one after the other. Then Sani began to relay his story.

"I have told you many times the story of our people's arrival to these cliffs. I told you of Spider Mother and of the Indian maiden and of the silken woven bridge that our people crossed to safety. I have told you of the wraith of Storm Spirit and also of the valiant heroics of Fire Spirit to save our people. The truth is that Fire Spirit is, in fact, my father. I am the son of Fire Spirit, and I have guarded and protected our people through the ages, appearing and reappearing in different ways to help our people. The truth is that I am much older than forty or forty-five, and I am discussing this secret with you tonight because there is a very grave situation at hand."

There was a silence for a moment as the medicine man let this new information sink in. He searched the faces of Kokopelli and Mai for disbelief or denial, but instead, the two young teens both watched him wide-eyed now and nodded their understanding.

"What is it you want to discuss with us?" asked Mai timidly.

"Kokopelli, do you remember the time that you followed the

wolves and when you were hurt?"

"Yes," said Kokopelli.

"That was no ordinary coincidence. That was planned and carried out by an evil creature we call a decayer. The night you were hurt, your mother, Shoshanna, entered into a pact with the decayer. Now, the evil creature has returned, and he seeks your younger brother Kai."

"What?" said Kokopelli and Mai in unison.

"Here, let me explain, and listen carefully to all I tell you. There is much about this world that is beyond basic understanding. Things are not always as they appear. You see, Mai, I know this information because I have informants in the village. They are guardian spirits that help me to protect all the people here. Do you understand?"

"Yes," they said, though they looked incredulously at Sani now.

"You see, Mai, when you were a small girl, I gifted you with a special kachina doll. You named him Yanaha, the brave one. All these years, your kachina doll was not just a gift but a special guardian to protect you and your family. He is magical and has the ability to communicate and even move. Mai, if you are not afraid now, I would like to reintroduce you to Yanaha."

And with that, the medicine man got up. He moved to the right corner of the adobe room and shifted a large basket away from the wall. He then stooped down to pull a partition of the wall away. What he revealed then to Kokopelli and Mai was a small tunnel; inside it, stood the doll, the kachina doll that belonged to Mai. It had two legs and two arms of red with a white cloth tunic embroidered with beautiful and intricate designs. It wore a vibrant yellow, green, and red headdress made of six feathers. Yanaha squinted always and had an upside-down frown, but in the present moment, the frown had turned into a little smile. Then, suddenly, Yanaha raised his left arm as if to wave.

"Mai, meet your magical guardian spirit, Yanaha." And Yanaha looked to Mai and Kokopelli. The kachina doll then moved out of the tunnel and into the room.

Both Kokopelli and Mai cried out in alarm and got to their feet in shock. They looked at each other and at Sani and at Yanaha with surprised expressions.

"He moves ... and talks!" exclaimed Mai.

"Yes. Yes, he does," said the medicine man. "Yanaha, please tell Kokopelli and Mai your story."

"At your service," began the little kachina doll gladly. He walked farther into the room and sat down cross-legged across from the two startled teenagers. "Please sit again," he instructed.

Together, the group of four now sat down.

"Yes, I have been your friend and guardian for a long time, Mai. I watched you grow. I watched your brother grow. I have been always by your side and have helped when needed to keep your family safe. But there is an issue of importance that we must discuss that makes me fear for your safety." And the little kachina doll then relayed to them the story of the night Kokopelli was hurt and of the visitation by the evil mountain lion spirit. When he was done explaining this, he then told them the story of the second visitation. He explained everything and left nothing out. The medicine man nodded his agreement.

"The decayers are from the third world. They crossed the bridge behind us. They are a smaller group, but they are powerful and dangerous. They have mostly left us alone over the years. We have kept an eye on their behaviors and whereabouts. There are other creatures that crossed the bridge as well that are our allies. We call them the ancient nature spirits. Together, we and the ancient nature spirits make certain the decayers stay away and leave our people alone. But recently, Hashkeh Naabah from the decayers has made these attempts to infiltrate our village and now plans to take your baby brother, Kai. It is our belief that this decayer means your brother great harm. You see, the decayers are an ancient group that engaged in the darkest black magic, witchcraft, and alchemy. They used experimentation on other creatures to develop their dark talents and rituals. They acquired the powers of shape-shifting into other animals through the use of black magic. They took these other creatures as vessels and used them for evil purposes. It is our belief that they intend to use Kai as a vessel. You see, the decayers are not able to transform completely human. They are humanlike with faceless visages and eyes like black voids. They have talons for hands and sharpened teeth, but they are not fully human. I believe they will take Kai to become human. When they do, they will attempt to overtake the village and perhaps destroy our people. Their hatred for our people has burned for eons. They are wicked and deceitful and full of cunning and malice. They can never be trusted. Do you understand?"

Kokopelli and Mai just nodded in disbelief, but they were trying hard to comprehend.

"Now, that brings me to you. Why would I tell you both such important and dangerous matters?" He looked at them and then slowly said, "because I need your help."

"Your mother, Shoshanna, intends to give Kai to Hashkeh Naabah in exchange for your lives as we discussed earlier. I know your mother would never wish to do this, but she has no choice. Therefore, it is our responsibility to intercept Kai and keep him from the clutches of the shape-shifters. This is a very important mission I am asking you to undertake. We must do everything in our power to keep the baby from the shape-shifters."

Kokopelli and Mai nodded and agreed to help. The party of four began to talk further into that night of what their plans for the future must be. It would be up to the medicine man,

Kokopelli, and Mai to rescue Kai. Meanwhile, the cliff village would be entrusted to the care of the kachina dolls and the medicine man's crow as a courier to the ancient nature spirit allies. If anything should happen, it would be up to the kachina dolls to protect the village. But for now, the three must rescue the baby Kai.

Chapter Three: A Narrow Escape

Kokopelli slipped his pet lizard into his satchel, asking Izou to stay out of sight. He touched Izou softly on his forehead, a sign of friendly affection. Izou settled into the satchel and quietly waited. Kokopelli and Mai descended from the cliffs and into the valley near dusk. Sani's instructions were clear. Wait for their mother to leave, grab their young brother, and run swiftly toward the waiting horses. The medicine man would meet them there beyond the fields. Together, they would ride east out of the valley and into the plains where the forests and mountains stretched beyond in the distance. Sani hoped that whomever followed would not track them farther than the stream and rocky crags that led into the deep forest. That was as far as the plan had gotten.

Kokopelli motioned silently to Mai to follow him down the trail and through the bushes beside the tall ponderosa pines. Together, they huddled amid the green leaves and stayed low to the ground. Mai shifted her satchel from her right to left hip, trying not to rustle the leaves. The darkness was coming. The moon had begun to make its ascent into the sky. Kokopelli squinted at the last rays of sunlight, perhaps twenty minutes of light left. He looked down into the dirt, listening for movements beyond the bush.

Soon, they heard muffled footsteps along the path. Their mother, Shoshanna, had come to deposit the baby beneath the first ponderosa pine. Through the bush, Mai and Kokopelli could make out the silhouette of her body. She was holding Kai, their brother. He appeared to be asleep. She cautiously looked left and right when she reached the pine. She was holding a buffalo hide bundle in her arms. It opened to reveal Kai bundled tightly in blankets. She looked again to the cliff dwelling and then to the distance. Kokopelli could barely discern the features of her face, which were set in deep concern. She looked down at Kai for a long moment. Beyond the pines, there was a sudden noise that frightened her. And then she heard it. Kokopelli and Mai heard it too—the low growling of a creature beyond.

"The decayers," Kokopelli whispered under his breath. "They're watching." Kokopelli looked through the bush leaves at the silhouette of his mother beside the tree and worried for her safety.

She set the child down at the base of the tree among the gnarled roots. She settled him into a spot between two deep roots where he could be well hidden to anyone. With sad eyes, she touched Kai again lovingly, setting his blankets around his face, and drew a fingertip lightly across his sleeping cheek. Then she straightened and hurried away toward the cliff village.

Kokopelli knew they must move fast. The plan was to snatch Kai and run as fast as they could. Both Kokopelli and Mai were good runners and had prepared well for a journey. Their sandals were snug and tight on their feet.

Kokopelli motioned again to Mai. They moved from the crouching position behind the bushes and rapidly moved toward the ponderosa pine, being careful to stay out of sight of the main trail. They had gotten within a few feet of the blankets and baby lying among the tree's roots when they halted at the noises again among the trees.

"She left the child as you wished," they heard the decayers say. There was a prowling sound among the trees, not just one but the movement of several beasts among the woods.

"Fetch him to me," a commanding voice ordered, deep and low, almost as if growling. Kokopelli recognized the low timber of the voice of the leader.

Meanwhile, Izou had slipped from the satchel to Kokopelli's sudden surprise and had darted from the bushes toward the sleeping baby.

"No, Izou!" a surprised Kokopelli mouthed, but it was too late. Mai also was shocked and rushed forward, tromping out of the bush to try to capture Izou. Izou crawled across the blankets, and his tail flicked across the face of Kai, forcing the baby abruptly awake with a sudden cry.

"Izou!" Kokopelli also rushed forward.

Mai tried to grab at Izou, but he moved fast out of her grasping fingers and back toward Kokopelli who promptly picked him up by the tail and dumped him into the satchel, securing it tightly this time. Meanwhile, Mai had scooped up Kai into her arms and was running already.

"Kokopelli!" she called anxiously over her shoulder. "Run!"

And the two took off in the growing dusk, knowing they only had a short distance to the horses. They burst into a sprint, barreling through the fields as fast as they could go, holding the baby, holding the satchels, and running for their lives.

Behind them, they could hear something was following ... To their dismay, it was not just one something but some creatures—several of them. Kokopelli looked over his shoulder to catch sight of three dire wolves off to the right. The Hyaenodon was in the lead within fifteen feet fast on his heels. He could not look to his left but sensed there were equal to or more creatures fast approaching on his heels.

"Kill them," he heard the Hyaenodon yell. He growled again menacingly.

At that, Kokopelli and Mai no longer looked back, knowing full well the predators could catch them. They ran into the tall corn fields. In amid the plants their feet pounded the dirt, their hearts beating wildly. Through the field and just beyond, the medicine man waited with the horses. They had to make it to the horses. The blades of corn plants whipped against their faces and arms and legs. They ran faster and faster toward the end of the field.

The wolves and lead creature were at their heels, growling

and barking. They were close—so close. They were closing in on Kokopelli and Mai. Kokopelli and Mai pushed through the last few rows of corn plants and out into the path. The horses were tethered ahead, but the medicine man ...

And then suddenly Sani was beside them. He pushed them both to the side, away from the cornstalks. Because he was the son of the Fire Spirit, he had the power to swiftly light fire from his hands. He propelled the fire towards the corn stalks which quickly burst into flames. Meanwhile, Kokopelli and Mai landed in the hard dirt. Mai rolled to the side on impact to shelter Kai from the fall. The baby was wailing and crying in a fit of fear. Kokopelli looked back to see the medicine man standing at the entrance to the burning corn field. His hands were upraised with red flashes of light. They emitted flames, more and more flames building that finally became a tremendously fast bonfire in the field of corn.

Kokopelli could hear the decayers. Instead of growling, they were yelping and rushing back from the fire. But when Kokopelli looked at the creature, the Hyaenodon, it was not moving amid the flames. It was not retreating. Rather, it just watched them with seething anger in its eyes. The fire did not appear to startle or frighten the Hyaenodon like the others. The others retreated. They moved back, prowling still, but the Hyaenodon watched them. The medicine man tried harder to send more fire into the bonfire, and then the Hyaenodon turned and quietly left. They heard it say, "Go, beyond the field to the east. Track them and return the baby to me."

"Quickly, we must leave!" The medicine man shouted to them. He lifted Mai from the ground and turned to help Kokopelli too. They ran to the horses, untethered them from the nearby branch, and swiftly mounted. Sani took the lead with Kokopelli and Mai following fast behind him. Sani held on to the reins of Mai's horse while she held tightly to the horse and also to the baby. They crossed into the plains at a full gait. Mai struggled to hold Kai and maintain control of her horse. They knew the dire wolves would continue to follow. The darkness was descending now. They crossed the plains and the stream. They traveled straight east, clamoring through the outskirts of the rocky crags and near the deep forest. And beyond this forest, they knew was the Snake River—the boundary they were told never to cross.

At the edge of the deep forest and amid the rocky crags of a hill past a steep ridge, the medicine man spotted an opening, perhaps a cave. He drew them onward up the rocky embankment. At this point, they had to get off the horses and led them by rope. They climbed the rocks of the hill to the opening. Mai again struggled with carrying Kai and getting up the rocks. Kokopelli took the ropes of her horse and his until they had reached the cave entrance.

"We should not enter the cave," called out Kokopelli, worried about what might be inside.

"We have no choice," said Sani. "Brave the cave, or fight those wolves—one or the other. It grows dark, and we cannot defend ourselves within the woods or out in the open. We'll have to risk it."

The medicine man stood before the dark entrance to the cave.

"I will be the one to enter firs—" He began but was startled by a sudden shadow movement within. The shadow creature grunted loudly not once but three times in warning. Suddenly, a large grizzly emerged out of the dark cave. The grizzly roared and stood on hind legs.

Meanwhile, in the distance behind them, the travelers could hear the howling of the predators upon the ridge not far from the rocky crag hill. Kokopelli, Mai, and Sani appeared to be trapped in a difficult predicament between the large grizzly bear and the wolves. The horses whinnied and neighed suddenly, bucking at the ropes. Kokopelli desperately tried to hold them as Mai held Kai tighter as he cried. The medicine man prepared to face the menacing grizzly himself.

"Halt!" came a loud voice from the forest. Just then, a stick on the ground from beyond amid the forest trees snapped. Several more snapped as a cloaked figure rushed forth toward them.

Meanwhile, Kai cried harder at the grizzly. The grizzly faced off with the medicine man. It roared but then halted and looked toward the cloaked figure. The grizzly dropped to its four legs. It grunted again—once, twice. The large bear moved toward the medicine man. Then the grizzly turned, brushing past Sani to head down the hill and toward the mysterious cloaked figure.

They were stunned by what had just happened. They looked to the cloaked stranger. His dark green cloak hood enshrouded his face. The horses were still bucking and neighing in fear of the grizzly, so the stranger reached a hand with a large green emerald ring on it toward the horses. A green orb of light emitted from the hand, and abruptly, the horses stopped. The grizzly had come close to the stranger's side, and so the stranger lowered his hood to reveal a dark-skinned bald head. He stared intently at the grizzly as if communicating with it, though no words were spoken.

"He speaks to the beasts with his mind," the medicine man said in awe.

Sani cleared his throat. "We want no harm. We have crossed the stream. We are crossing the rocky crags and going into the forest to hide from these wolves. We are from the cliff village. We need assistance. Are you friend or foe?"

"Ha-ha," the stranger chuckled softly. The bear sat tamely beside him. The horses quieted, and yet the exhausted baby was crying weakly. "Friend or foe? Well, that depends, I suppose, on you. Why are you here? And why are the decayers following you?" And with that, he motioned past them to the ridge where the dire wolves prowled again. One howled, and the others pick up the howling in unison. There was a pack above them on the ridge overlooking the rocky crags and hillside cave.

"We are fleeing the wolves with this child," Mai explained. "He is my brother, Kai. They meant to have him."

"Ah, yes. I know," said the stranger softly.

"You know?"

"Yes, I have been tracking your movements myself since you left the village." He smiled at them. His eyes glowed yellow and green.

"How? How do you even know us? Who are you?" Kokopelli demanded. He found a nearby stick to defend himself and the others if need be. "Speak! Who are you?"

The stranger patted the head of the grizzly bear beside him. He appeared to communicate something to the bear, and the bear turned off into the forest. "You know, he was not happy to find you in his home. He's naturally quite a kind fellow, but you humans shocked him to say the least. He was merely defending himself from perceived intruders. I explained to him your predicament, and he has decided to graciously allow you to stay in his cave for a night ... to keep those predators ... decayers, " he muttered. "To keep the decayers away from the child.

"Now forgive me. Where are my manners?" He chuckled. "I am the one you call the Earth Spirit, oh great one, ha-ha ... My name is Tsintah." He briefly bowed. "And you, Sani, look so much like your father, Fire Spirit."

The medicine man's jaw dropped open. He was so startled he did not know what to say.

Mai came forward with the struggling Kai who continued to whimper and cry. Exasperated, she said, "Without milk, he'll grow hungry. How will we keep him living? How will we keep from the wolves? How will we be able to do any of this?"

"We'll have to figure a way to feed your little brother. He'll need nourishment soon, or he will continue to cry," said Sani.

"Sani and Kokopelli, use your talents to build a swift fire at the entrance to the cave. We rest here tonight," said Tsintah. "And now to help with the child."

Tsintah raised his ringed hand toward Kai. Again, a green orb of light emitted from his fingers. The baby stopped crying. He blinked twice and then fell into a slumber. Mai looked at Tsintah, amazed. Tsintah merely smiled and then shrugged. "One of my many talents—the ability to communicate via mind with animals. Of course, I cannot communicate with decayers like those on the ridge. Yet, have you not noticed that the howls have ceased? They sense that I am here. They know that I am here. And they are afraid—deeply afraid ... as they should be."

Above them on the ridge, there was nothing but eerie silence. The travelers set to work on their encampment at the entrance. The medicine man ordered the others to quickly gather twigs and limbs and kindling. He assembled a tripod of dry nettles and limbs and then whispered a few ancient words over them. He reached forth his hands again, and sudden sparks glowed red into the nettles, catching swiftly ablaze. Sani worked quickly to build the blaze as Mai, Kokopelli, and Tsintah kept watch over the ridge and the sleeping baby.

Once the fire was built, the medicine man straightened up. He looked overhead at the half moon in the sky. "Do not worry about the wolves now." He reassured the others. "They will stay back from fire for certain."

"As I said, they fear me more than they fear that fire," said Tsintah quietly. "Now, to help you with the child." He reached into his green cloak to reveal a drinking pouch. Mai held Kai in her arms as he rested, and Tsintah stepped toward them now. Mai stepped back, looked at the others, and then stepped forward in trust toward Tsintah.

"Not exactly mother's milk, but this will have to do for the journey," he stated matter-of-factly.

"Journey?" Kokopelli asked. He again raised the stick in his hand.

"Yes, of course," said Tsintah. "The journey to free your father." He nodded at Sani. "The time has finally come." He nodded again at the medicine man.

"But how?" asked Sani.

"Well, first, you will clearly need my assistance. I have been watching you for a long time. I always keep my distance, as I did not want to enrage the Storm Spirit, but clearly, the time has come to step in, to pick a side, and well ..." He smiled and turned. He squatted before the fire, throwing a piece of wood into the blaze. "I have a soft heart for underdogs—always have, always will." He smiled again but then looked sad for a moment. "I have missed Ahiga."

"Settle down tonight to rest. The decayers will not bother us tonight," he muttered. "Decayers," he mumbled under his breath like a curse. "Feed this to Kai, and then you three must rest for the long journey ahead. I will keep watch over the darkness."

Mai woke her brother Kai and then opened the drinking pouch. "Milk?" she asked.

"The drinking pouch is magical and will always remain filled," Tsintah noted.

Mai used the pouch to feed Kai. The baby hesitated at first but drank thirstily.

"It resembles mother's milk and will nourish him." Tsintah smiled.

The medicine man then motioned to the others to bed down near the fire. Once again, the medicine man whispered to the blaze, and it leapt anew, higher and higher until all were warm inside the cave.

"Sleep." The medicine man nodded to Kokopelli and Mai.

Mai placed the satiated babe beside her on the ground and

closed her eyes to rest. Kokopelli, still holding the stick, looked again at the silent ridge and then to the forest. There was nothing but silence and the crackling of the fire. This amused Tsintah and the medicine man nodded to him again.

"Rest," the medicine man said. "You will need your endurance for the arduous trek ahead."

Kokopelli and Mai lay close to each other and closed their eyes. The Earth Spirit raised his ringed hand briefly their way again, and they began to slumber.

"Tsintah, you do us a great honor. We are indebted to you," Sani began.

The medicine man placed his hand on his heart.

"I couldn't remain uninvolved much longer. As you know, the threat of the decayers grows day by day. You and I both know what Storm Spirit must do if they succeed," said Tsintah.

"Storm Spirit," muttered Sani.

"I have chosen to assist you only to defeat the decayers. If word circles back to Haseya that I have meddled with human affairs, there may be grave repercussions." The Earth Spirit stirred up the fire. "This ground is quite hard," he stated. He raised his hand to the earth around him. A green light sparked from his hand, causing grass roots to suddenly sprout and spread all around them in the cave.

"Ah, I am well pleased by this." He laughed and clapped his hands. "Well pleased indeed." The Earth Spirit gently lifted the satchel from Kokopelli and let loose the tiny lizard in the pouch.

"I am certain you have been trapped in there long enough." He lifted Izou and looked into his eyes. "You are quite the troublemaker aren't you, my little lizard?" He looked at Izou mischievously and then released the lizard to the ground.

The lizard settled into the grass beside the Earth Spirit. A berry plant raised from the earth to their right as well.

"Blueberries of the forest." Tsintah smiled and picked a few. He held the berries out to Sani and placed one in front of the lizard, Izou. Izou began eating the blueberry hungrily. "A gift. You all must be quite famished."

They sat in the darkness of the cave with the shadows of the fire dancing across their faces. Tsintah reached into the pouch again to find Kokopelli's flute.

"Ah, I do love music. Humans have such wonderful abilities."

Sani nodded.

"You must journey past the Snake River tomorrow," said Tsintah pointedly.

"Past the river? But no, the Spider Mother said never to cross!"

"But you must." Tsintah looked at the sleeping baby. "It is the only way. Your father is out there ... past the river. I suppose Spider Mother neglected to tell you that part."

"No, she did not mention that part," muttered Sani.

"It will be a dangerous trek. At the river, you will encounter your first test."

"Test? What do you mean, Tsintah?" Sani questioned.

"I also have a limited gift of foresight, and I see three tests in your path—each test more difficult than the next. When I leave, I will provide you a map and compass, but you must complete these tasks alone. I cannot be seen with you. Upon completion of the third trial, I will return to you with a gift." The Earth Spirit rose abruptly, adjusting his hood. He seemed to look directly into the woods, listening carefully to the forest.

"One final warning," he said. "There are many dangers past the Snake River, but you already know this ... One danger I speak of is here now—with us. It does not affect me, as I am immortal. They ..." He pointed to the forest beyond the cave. "They are always in the woods, always watching and waiting ... Beware of these ... lurkers, the dark watchers. These are the silent ones watching in the woods of the wilderness." He looked back into the woods thoughtfully, looking all around and sensing their presence, sensing something but not fully explaining it to Sani. "This presence I call the lurkers ... You must ignore them in the wilderness at all costs. You may feel them near by the tingling of the hair on the back of your neck. You may feel that something is watching your travel party. You are right. You must ignore it at all costs. They are not the decayers. They are ... something else ... quite ominous. Do not look at them."

He looked into the woods and mumbled, "Ghosts of the forest." He then looked back at the medicine man. "Do not make eye contact with the ghosts, the dark watchers. Understood?"

"Yes." The medicine man watched the Earth Spirit cautiously. He wanted to look into the woods, but he knew he must not. *Ghosts of the forest*, he thought to himself.

"Good, then that is all. Now get some rest. I will keep watch tonight. Tomorrow you cross the Snake River. Be on your guard. When you wake, you will find that I am gone. I will leave the map and compass. You must rise early and get your travel companions and horses to the river before the dire wolves encircle your party. Be fast. Fly."

The Earth Spirit raised his bejeweled hand, and with that, the medicine man lay onto the grass as well and rested. The Earth Spirit continued to stoke the fire. He ate some berries, petted Izou, and eventually returned him to Kokopelli's satchel.

Every now and then, the Earth Spirit stopped and glanced to the dark woods, examining them with a look of mild concern. "Ghosts of the forest," he muttered to himself, feeling their lurking presence in the dark shadows.

Chapter Four: An Angry Warrior

Hashkeh Naabah was fiercely wrathful. He crossed the lands to the west with two dire wolves at his heels, following behind his rapid gait. He furiously hurled himself through the forests and hills and across the canyon lands. He was so enraged that he was shifting into his original humanoid self, an entity neither human nor fully creature. Over the centuries, he had become a beast of the darkness. He practiced the blackest witchcraft, and so his body had begun to resemble his soul, decayed and faceless. His eyes were black pits, and his hands were mangled with clawed fingers. His flesh clung to his bones and appeared lifeless and decayed. He was a shape-shifter. As he ran, both he and the other two shape-shifter witches behind him began to morph. They climbed the steep rocky hill that led to Rattlesnake Ridge overlooking the decayer lair below.

As they ran, a large rattlesnake, both venomous and stealthy, coiled on the rock path and began to rattle loudly. It hissed to three other rattlesnakes within the vicinity, and they took up the rattling noise. Hashkeh Naabah recognized them as his scouts, other shape-shifters from the community, and so he propelled himself over the first rattlesnake, and the other shape-shifters followed closely behind. As he crossed over and continued onward, the three rattlesnake bodies also morphed into similar humanoid creatures. And the three joined the party, running now to the lair.

They crested the ridge and ran down the path. Along either side were tall spikes. At the top of the spikes rested the skulls of buffalo and deer. The spikes led down the path to the giant hogan made of deadwood timber. On either side of the path were the tar pits, ominous and dark and bubbly and deadly. Here, there were no trees except the gnarled and leafless kind, as twisted and dark as the inhabitants of this land.

The decayer community was quite large. The shape-shifters had experimented on many animals over the years and recruited many more creatures to their ranks in dark ritualistic fashion. There were many wigwam structures nearby, also made of deadwood. Torches lit the community grounds, and in front of the giant hogan, there were three decayers in humanoid shape field dressing a deer they had killed. They had turned the deer upside down and hoisted it to a tree where the blood pooled on the ground below. They were in the midst of cutting when the party of decayers led by Hashkeh Naabah exploded into the camp. Enraged and furious, the Hyaenodon leader cuffed and tossed to the side all three decayers. He pulled sharply on the deer and snapped the tree limb. The dead deer fell into his arms, and he growled ferociously and lifted it overhead. He threw it hard against the wall of the hogan.

This behavior attracted the attention of many more decayers, and he went into the hogan shelter in a rage. As he went, he bellowed, "Call the twenty now! I have need to speak to them immediately."

Word quickly was dispatched through the village, and it was not long before the twenty most ancient shape-shifters, the decayed ones who crossed the silken bridge so many years ago, entered the Hogan as well to sit in council with Hashkeh Naabah. There was one particular of the twenty named Neqael. He was most reluctant to enter the Hogan, but he did as commanded. No one ever crossed Hashkeh Naabah without facing dire consequences.

"The plans have been sabotaged. The boy and girl have run off with the baby! I ordered the wolf pack to follow in their pursuit," said Hashkeh Naabah.

The twenty looked across to each other but were careful to remain quiet until addressed again.

"I need the boy to become human myself. We cannot do this ritual without a live human baby. It does not work any other way! And our plans to infiltrate the village ... They have failed."

And he growled, low and ominous. He prowled the floor back and forth. There were cages of animals as well in the hogan, and those animals were all silent and watching, fearful of the shape-shifters.

The humanoid creature walked over to a cage of birds. He examined them carefully, and then took the smallest, most delicate one. And he proceeded to eat it head first, crunching loudly on its bones. He tossed the remaining carcass to the ground.

He then smiled cunningly and deceitfully. "We will continue our plan nevertheless to become humans. Rather than infiltrate the village, we must now attack the village head-on and kidnap the inhabitants. We will use them as our vessels. It will take time to prepare our ranks. We will need weapons. We will take every shape-shifter to attack the village. In the meantime, the wolves will bring me back the baby. Go now, and prepare for me the plans," he said curtly to the twenty before dismissing them.

As they began to clear out, Hashkeh Naabah motioned to the last councilmember, the one named Neqael. "You," he said. "Come here. We have much to discuss privately."

And Neqael reluctantly agreed to follow his leader's directions.

Chapter Five: Snake Charmer

Kokopelli woke to the feeling of something warm against his back. He reached behind him and felt a thick matte of fur. Thinking it was his buffalo hide from home, he began to pull at it to cover himself. But when he heard a loud grunt, his eyes flew open wide. Whatever it was, it was something alive and quite warm. He blinked at Mai and the baby across from him, both still sleeping, and when he rolled over to see the looming mass of the giant grizzly, he swiftly moved back in fear. Scrambling to his feet and away from the bear, he watched it worriedly. The bear, however, was sitting still at the entrance to the cave with its back to Kokopelli and the others. It was silently watching the ridge. Kokopelli looked to the ridge to where he saw the wolf pack prowling. There appeared to be five of them, and even from here, he could see they were quite large.

"Decayers," he mumbled.

Kokopelli then looked around to the others. Mai snuggled close to Kai who had awakened from his movement and was just watching Kokopelli expectantly. The fire was out and was just embers now, and the medicine man was near the side wall of the cave. He seemed to be examining a large object. Kokopelli moved closer to see the item had symbols and drawings on it. On the hide leather, their cave was mapped. From there, he saw a long, solid red line leading northeast across a wide river and into a mountainous area.

"This is the map Tsintah spoke of last night," said Sani. "This will be our path. Look at the three spots marked with burned smudges. These must be the locations we must journey to as Tsintah explained ... the three tests he mentioned." He pointed to the first smudge that was on the river, and there appeared to be a symbol of a waterfall at that location. He looked at it thoughtfully. Further down the river was a symbol of a crossing area, maybe a bridge or boat, and Kokopelli wondered why the path took them across the waterfall and not farther down to the other location.

Kokopelli looked at Sani. "Tests?"

"Yes, you were asleep. He explained much to me. He said we are to travel quickly through the forest to the Snake River. We must cross it."

Kokopelli looked at the medicine man in alarm.

"Yes," Sani continued. "Tsintah left this backpack and spear by the wall. I awoke and found food and a container for water inside. Wake your sister and brother quickly. We don't have much time. The bear keeps watch, but it will not be long before the decayers have discovered Tsintah is gone. Now eat."

And with that, the medicine man handed jerky to Kokopelli. He gave Kokopelli the drinking pouch for Kai, and Kokopelli woke Mai. They sat down cross-legged to eat fast, and after Mai was finished, she began feeding Kai from the drinking pouch.

The bear grunted from the entrance of the cave and made a sudden movement to his feet. He growled menacingly and then sat down again. He huffed a few times more.

The medicine man was still looking at this thing called a map and further examining the shiny metal piece in his hand called a compass. It was foreign to him. It had an arrow inside that pointed toward the forest and said *E*.

"This means east," he said after having looking at the map compass key. "That is the way we must go and soon."

They gathered their gear together. The medicine man reached into the backpack and gave Mai something from inside it. It flashed in the sun.

"A dagger ... a gift from Tsintah. He said we would encounter dangers."

The medicine man then gave the spear to Kokopelli. "I presume you know how to use one of these from your hunting trips?"

Kokopelli nodded.

"Good," said Sani. "Very good." And he tousled Kokopelli's hair briefly.

Kokopelli helped Mai to secure Kai tightly to her as she had seen her mother and other women of the tribe carrying babies to their chests wrapped in a large blanket tied at the back.

"I want your hands to be free," explained Kokopelli, smiling.

The bear began to pace the cave floor eagerly. He grunted and growled. Kokopelli went to the entrance of the cave, followed by Mai and Kai. The medicine man was already in the valley below. Overnight, a natural spring had risen to the surface just below the rocky crags where the horses were drinking.

"Tsintah, thank you," whispered Kokopelli under his breath. The wind came up then. Kokopelli faintly thought he heard on the wind a voice saying, "Go!"

And then he remembered. Turning instantly, he said to Mai, "Izou? Where is Izou?"

He reached for his satchel. Izou was inside already, but the flute was missing. Mai rushed with Kai down the crags to the horses where the medicine man was helping her to mount and in turn, mounted his own horse. He held tightly to the rein of her horse.

"Kokopelli! We must go! Now!"

The bear roared from the cave entrance and flew down the rocky crag as the riders prepared to leave. Kokopelli remained for an instant. He was checking his clothes for his flute when he found it tied by a thin rope around his neck. Tsintah must have secured it there last night. Odd that he would put Izou in the pouch but not the flute. But no matter, he had no time to think further, as the bear roared again. Kokopelli could see then that the dire wolves were descending from the ridge into their valley. There was no time. He ran to his horse, thinking of the wolves, thinking of the bear that now stood on hind legs, displaying its massive power and strength to the predators ahead.

No! he thought. *He can't fight them alone.* But then Kokopelli heard the voice more urgent this time in the wind. It said one word: "Go!"

The medicine man and Mai, holding tightly to Kai, were already heading into the deep forest along the narrow footpath. They were kicking their horses into full gait into the forest, and Kokopelli, in turn, got onto his horse and swung toward the path. Behind him, he could hear the grizzly ferociously roaring. The bear was now blocking the path behind them, preventing the predators from following. The bear was standing on hind legs and he was buying them some time to get to the river.

Kokopelli's horse raced into the forest behind Sani and Mai with Kai. The medicine man yelled back to Mai and Kokopelli over the sound of the galloping hooves. "Keep your eyes on me! Do not look into the forest. Keep your eyes on me!" And that was all that he could get out as the horses raced deeper and deeper into the trees. The undergrowth of the forest was thick on either side of the narrow path, and branches from time to time whipped at them. On a few occasions, they had to barely evade low-hanging branches and slow down to skirt other fallen trees on the path. Yet, overall, they flew as fast as they could through the forest. Mai held Kai tightly to her while trying to maintain her balance on the horse. The medicine man clutched the reins to her horse, and Kokopelli held tightly the spear and his satchel with Izou inside.

They rode for a good hour and a half, the horses never tiring, keeping their pace. Occasionally, Kokopelli thought he could hear the howling of the wolves far, far off in the distance. He worried for the grizzly, but he kept going. Mai held tightly to Kai and kept her eyes on the back of the medicine man as ordered, although she thought she saw something out of the corner of her eye once. She saw something dark amid the woods off to her left. She thought it was another animal. She wanted to look, but she didn't. Whatever it was, it made her shiver. And then, it was gone.

They reached the embankment of the river. The medicine man got off his horse and quietly led them onward. He moved forward to the water. He looked at the wide expanse of the river—too far and too deep at this area to cross with the horses. He noticed the water current was moving rapidly. He scanned the other embankment for movements and saw none. As he stood there still wondering what to do and whether to check the map, he heard a distant thundering. It did not cease, and he realized the thundering was the sound of water falling. The river ... the waterfall. Sani then told them to alight from their horses, and he pointed down river with the flow of the current. They began to follow the embankment down the river to the thundering noise that grew louder and louder. They knew they did not have much time to figure out a plan to cross, as the wolves would be tracking them. They had to put some distance in between.

The thundering grew to a roaring of water descending off the cliff ahead. They continued on warily, watching the river and watching the other embankment.

At the cliff's edge, the water rushed over. It poured in one great gush down and down, farther to the ground where the river swelled out into a little pool and continued onward off into the distance. At the cliff's edge on their side was a makeshift wooden structure tethered by ropes to the trees. The structure held a series of ladders and platforms that led to the ground surface below. And in the pool, they realized at once that they were not alone.

The waterfall pounded heavily into the pool. It was loud and thunderous. At the base, not ten feet from this on the east embankment, was the wreckage of a broken wagon. And near the busted remains, on the embankment, was a child. The child wore a gingham dress and had blonde hair. Her clothes were muddied, and she was turned from them, collapsed and appearing to sob into her hands on the embankment. There was no one else at the waterfall, just the child.

The medicine man handed the reins of his horse to Mai. They tethered the horses to nearby branches. Mai stayed behind with the gear, with the backpack and satchels and Kai. Kokopelli left the spear behind with Mai, and both the medicine man and Kokopelli swiftly descended the ladders of the structure until they reached the ground. The child was still sobbing, her face turned away from them. The child was on the other embankment.

They stepped into the cold pool of water. Behind them the water beat into the river from the falls, causing ripples and waves and mist to rise. They walked farther into the pool, deeper and deeper until they had crossed halfway. The water was to their waists. As Sani neared the wreckage of the wagon, he headed for the child. The child suddenly stopped sobbing into her hands. She lifted her head, her blonde curls about her face. Then she turned her head to look directly at them. Her eyes were black and slit like a snake's, and she opened her mouth not to cry but to expose snake fangs. Sani stopped in sudden alarm, as did Kokopelli. The water continued to thunder behind them and from the wreckage of the wagon slithered out a multitude of black snakes.

"Water moccasins!" warned the medicine man.

The girl on the embankment was no longer collapsed but standing and approaching the water, smiling at them with glistening black snake eyes and fangs exposed.

Sani and Kokopelli stepped backward, retreating toward the falls, but from behind them through the falls, they heard a great hissing. They looked back in time to see a giant viper emerge from the waters, massive as a dragon. Kokopelli faced the giant viper from the falls, and the medicine man turned to face the child and the water moccasins piling one over another by a hundred or more out of the wagon. Now the child with the viper face was wading into the water toward them behind the mass of slithering black snacks. She was pleased at their dire circumstances.

They were trapped. The medicine man did the only thing he could think to do. He could not use fire, but he reached both hands deep into the water in front of him as the throng of water moccasins moved toward them. And he used his fire strength to boil the water ahead of him, blocking the water moccasins. The water boiled and bubbled violently, and now the water moccasins were not just slithering across the water. They were writhing viciously in one great mass of black just outside the boiling line. They could not cross.

Meanwhile, Kokopelli had no weapons. He had left the dagger and spear overhead. He had nothing at all to protect himself from the giant viper moving massively overhead from the falls, threatening to devour them. He only had one thing; all he could do was reach for the flute tied by rope to his neck. He thought to himself quickly. *There must be some reason Tsintah wanted this on me.* And as the viper lowered its pitted face and slit eyes to stare directly within two feet of Kokopelli, Kokopelli brought the flute to his lips. The snake's mouth began to open, revealing enormous razor-sharp fangs. Kokopelli closed his eyes in the mist and began to play. He thought he would die. He waited to die. He waited for the viper to strike, but it did not. Kokopelli kept playing, and the snake slowly closed its mouth and watched curiously. The tune continued.

Meanwhile, overhead, Mai was frantically and helplessly watching in horror the scene below her. Izou rushed out of his pouch and past her feet at that moment and moved toward the ropes securing the wooden structure. He appeared to be gnawing at the cords of the rope, which gave Mai an idea. She fumbled quickly into the backpack, reaching for the dagger and then followed Izou's lead, attempting to cut the cords that held the wooden structure in place.

The music still played, the giant viper still watched curiously, and the water still thundered around below. The medicine man began slowly advancing toward the mass of water moccasins, boiling the water and forcing the water moccasins toward the snake girl. She realized instantly what could happen. She hissed and bared her fangs again and attempted to swim out and away. But it was too late. The mass of water moccasins overtook her abruptly, turning on their master. They pulled her down, biting and writhing and biting and writhing—a great mass of slithering black over her as she reached one solitary arm out from under the water. And now she was under the water, and the medicine man was driving them all farther and farther down away from Kokopelli through the magic of fire and boiling water.

Kokopelli played. He did not know what else to do. The giant viper was now inches from his face and slowly opening its mouth. Kokopelli closed his eyes, preparing to die. From above, the great wooden structure rocked and creaked, and he opened his eyes to see Mai with Kai pushing against the structure. Suddenly, it fell over and onto the great snake. It broke and busted over the snake and forced the snake down momentarily, stunning it and also making it violently mad. And now, Mai tossed the spear into the water near Kokopelli, and he swam for it. The snake burst through the busted wood and rose higher and higher up the waterfall to where Mai holding Kai, alarmed and suddenly terribly frightened, stood.

Kokopelli now had the spear, and he straightened himself and launched it at the snake head with all his might as he had seen his father do on hunting trips. The spear hit its mark and went through the underjaw and throat of the snake. The snake shuddered and fell into the water, writhing. The great fall caused a wave of water to knock over Kokopelli, and when he came up from the water, he saw the medicine man standing on the embankment sending fire from his hands to burn the dying, writhing, and hissing snake. Kokopelli quickly swam out of the water and onto the embankment. Mai and

Izou watched from above with great relief. Kai was crying again.

The snakes were gone. The great viper was dead and burning. The test was defeated, but there was a slight problem they soon realized.

Mai, Izou, Kai, and the horses were on the cliff with the dire wolves swiftly tracking and advancing, and Sani and Kokopelli were too far below, at the base of the waterfall, with no way to reach the others.

Chapter Six: At the Water's Edge

Mai looked down at Kai. He was nestled close to her still. She scooped up Izou and shouted down to Sani and to Kokopelli.

"I can't get down, especially with the horses. I don't know what to do." She looked over at the horses tethered to the branches nearby.

Below, Kokopelli was attempting to scale the cliff, but there were no strong footholds to climb much higher. The medicine man was looking across to the other embankment.

"It's not as steep on the other side. If we can figure a way to get you across ..." he stated. He paused talking when he noticed that the water from the falls had suddenly frozen in place. He looked up ahead at the top of the falls in great alarm.

"Well this is quite a predicament we find ourselves in," came a voice from behind Mai as she stood near the cliff's edge.

Mai also froze and slowly looked over her shoulder. The voice had come from a distance behind her, and she followed the sound to the middle of the quickly frozen river.

"Tsintah mentioned you mortals may need my help. I was reluctant, but now I see ... We are in quite the pinch."

A woman in a long, flowing white dress with blue embroidery was walking upon the frozen water—actually walking upon the water in the middle of the river. Her beautiful dark hair flowed over her shoulders and down her back.

"And I surmise that you are Mai," she stated matter-of-factly as she continued to walk toward Mai. She came to stand near Mai, nearly at the edge of the cliff. The water beneath her, that had rushed wildly into the falls, was now completely still. She stood there nonplussed by the frozen current beneath.

"And this must be Kai." She smiled briefly.

"Yes," said Mai hesitantly.

"Well, we don't have much time then. Tell the others to meet you in the forest at the mountain stream. It is across the river and a mile's trek east. I'll help you to cross."

"But how?"

"Never mind how. You'll see soon enough. Now tell the others. We don't have much time. The wolves tracking you are close upon us."

Mai did as she was ordered, yelling down to Kokopelli and the medicine man. "I have found a way to cross. Don't worry. We'll be all right. I need you to trust me. Cross the river to the other side and meet me at the mountain stream. It is one mile's trek east. Just trust me."

Kokopelli and Sani both looked inquisitively at Mai. At that, Mai added, "A woman has come to help me."

"What woman?" asked Kokopelli, on guard for his sister.

"Tahoma," answered the woman softly to Mai. "My name is Tahoma."

"She said her name is Tahoma."

Water Spirit, said the medicine man to himself, startled. And he began to tug Kokopelli from the base of the cliff. Once again, the water picked up and the current rushed down the falls. Tahoma continued to stand on the rushing water as if it were solid.

"We'll do as she says. Come on. We have to hurry and cross!" yelled Sani.

"But ... who is this?" demanded Kokopelli as they started to cross the flowing water again, being careful to skirt the wreckage below the falls.

"We'll see soon enough." And that is all the medicine man

offered in explanation.

Meanwhile, on the cliff, Tahoma had moved again to the center of the river. She slowly raised her hands out and away from her sides, and as she did, the water around her began to rise up and form a tunnel. In the tunnel, Mai could see the exposed wet river rocks. Waters, murky and wild, rose solidly around the tunnel to nearly eight feet high. Tahoma's hands were now over her head, and then she looked at Mai directly.

"Untie the horses, and they will cross the dry river bottom themselves. You gather your belongings and the child and also cross swiftly!"

Mai did again as she was ordered, loosening the ropes for the horses and watched as they stepped out onto the wet rocks carefully one by one, beginning to work their way across the river tunnel. Mai quickly grabbed the dagger and put it in the backpack, slinging the pack and satchels around her right shoulder. She held tightly to the packs and to Kai with her left hand, hoping and praying that she would not fall on the slippery rocks near the waterfall's edge. She too began to follow the horses across. Mai refused to look around the water tunnel. Her heart pounded as she carefully moved one step after the other, making her way across to the other embankment. The horses were already ahead of her and heading into the forest, and as she stepped off the last rock, she breathed a sigh of relief. She looked down at Kai who was awake and beginning to fuss. He needed changing and food, but wolves were near so she continued on.

"Not as difficult as it seems," said the strange woman beside her now. Mai looked back to where the woman had stood. The solid tunnel through heavy water was still raised eight feet high, but Tahoma stood next to her, reaching out to soothe the baby.

"Come. We don't have much time. Kai is getting hungry." The woman placed a hand upon Mai's back and motioned to her to follow the horses. "To the mountain stream. You will see. A place to recoup."

"But the wolves ..." began Mai. Tahoma and Mai were now walking side by side into the deep, thick greenery of the surrounding forest. "Ah, the wolves." Tahoma smiled bemusedly. She continued to walk beside Mai with her hand at Mai's back. When they had walked near to fifty feet from the river, in the distance behind them, the dire wolves had broken out of the woods across the Snake River and were cautiously examining the eight-foot tunnel of water. Tahoma and Mai continued to walk slowly. Mai was completely unaware of the wolves' arrival, but Tahoma, though she continued to walk, raised her other hand into the air briefly. Two wolves had begun to cross the wet river bottom through the tunnel surrounded by rushing river water. Three others stayed back on the river's edge, waiting to see what would happen. Tahoma continued to walk with Mai and the baby, and she smiled to herself ever so slightly. Then the fingers of her other hand made a sudden pattern in the air. The tunnel suddenly gushed together with tremendous speed and voracity, taking out the two wolf scouts that had been attempting to cross.

Mai looked at Tahoma briefly, wondering why she had moved her fingers and as she started to look behind her, Tahoma interrupted her by saying, "Come on, dear! We've got to catch up to the others." Tahoma was smiling.

The Snake River in the far distance had now returned to normal as if nothing had happened. The two wolves were gone. The three wolves seemed to move from side to side several times before retreating back the way they had come.

"Those wolves won't bother us, as you know. We've crossed the river, and now we can rest some before you continue the journey."

Meanwhile, not too far off from this travel party, Sani and Kokopelli were also advancing through the thick foliage of the forest. They were nearing what they hoped to be the mountain stream when they came across a small secluded glen. Kokopelli was walking forward when he sensed something off to his right. He had this odd feeling about it; the hair on his neck rose for an instant; and he could have sworn he was seeing some dark entity in the forest. Wondering if his mind was playing tricks on him or if he had come across some dangerous animal, he moved back and to the left, preparing to look full on at the creature.

A hand slapped down hard on his shoulder, jolting him. "Don't look! Look away," said Sani behind him.

Kokopelli did not understand. Is this what the medicine man had been speaking of earlier on the forest ride? What was this? He began to peer over to his right.

"No! Close your eyes. It's a ghost or ghoul. They are called lurkers. They are spirits or entities in the forest that have not moved on. If you look, they take you. Close your eyes. Don't look!"

Kokopelli looked behind him at the medicine man briefly. Sani's eyes were now looking at the forest floor around them. The dark presence in the woods, a mass of darkness as far as he could tell out of the corner of his eye, was waiting for something—perhaps waiting for them to look. Instead, Kokopelli followed Sani's eyes to the ground. There, swarming at their feet, were many insects. Spiders, night crawlers, beetles, cockroaches, and centipedes crawled all around them and were starting to crawl up their legs. Kokopelli began to swat at a centipede crawling up his calf muscle.

"Don't move," said the medicine man again, now firmly squeezing Kokopelli's shoulder. "Don't move; don't look. These crawlers, decomposing creatures, are attracted to the presence of the lurkers. Close your eyes."

And Kokopelli did. He stood very still.

Up ahead, concurrently, Mai and Tahoma had come to the mountain stream. It appeared to be in a valley at the base of the rising hills leading to snowcapped mountain peaks in the distance. Mai thought this place was absolutely beautiful.

"I like this place," said Mai to Tahoma.

"Yes, it is nice," said Tahoma simply.

The horses were already drinking in the stream, and their tails whipped back and forth. Tahoma led Mai and Kai to a moss-covered area of rocks. Mai set her pack down and checked on Kai. Together, Tahoma and Mai undid the snug blanket so they could get Kai fed and changed. This place seemed peaceful to Mai but even more so in the presence of Tahoma who had a mothering, protective quality to her. They sat for a while with the baby until Tahoma frowned.

"They should have been here by now." She scanned the forest with her eyes. Tahoma stood up and brushed off her dress.

"I think I should go check up on them. I believe they may be in that direction." She pointed downstream into the forest. "Mai, I'm going to leave you here for a bit with Kai and the horses. This is a safe place. You should be all right. I've got to go find them," she suddenly said with urgency.

And with that, Tahoma hurried into the forest, downstream from Mai and Kai.

Kokopelli and the medicine man still stood in the forest. They could feel the insects and crawlers. They could hear every noise around them with a heightened sense, adrenaline gushing into their bloodstreams. Sani still held tightly to Kokopelli.

"We'll have to move forward with our eyes closed. The crawlers are still here, which means that thing is still here in the woods waiting. We'll have to move forward slowly, one foot in front of the other," said the medicine man.

And just like that, one foot in front of the other and stumbling here and there, the two began to move forward again toward the mountain stream. Yet, they had no idea how much longer it would take, and at the pace they were traveling, this was dangerous. As far as they knew, the dire wolves were still tracking their party.

"Keep going," encouraged Sani.

Kokopelli stumbled on the undergrowth of the forest. He tripped, falling forward and suddenly opening his eyes to catch himself before hitting the earth.

The medicine man lost his grip on Kokopelli and reached out alarmedly. "Kokopelli! Kokopelli!"

But Kokopelli was not answering because he had looked up from the earth floor to see something coming fast toward him—a woman. She had long, flowing locks of hair that cascaded in the wind, and her white dress billowed behind her as she ran. Her right hand reached for her necklace. The pendant seemed to be made of glass or crystal, and it glowed bright blue. She gripped the necklace, and a shockwave as hard as a water wave permeated the air, and with it, flashed a brilliant blue light.

Even with his eyes closed, Sani could see under his eyelids the brightness of the light, but the shockwave is what tossed him back to the ground. His eyes flew open to see Kokopelli thrown as well. The woman, whomever she was, was standing in the clearing, still gripping her necklace and looking directly at the lurker. The medicine man surmised that the light and shockwave startled the lurker and caused it to retreat, but he kept his eyes on the woman. Kokopelli was doing the same. Both of them were startled but also relieved.

The woman then looked at them. "Well, are you going to stay there forever, or are you going to follow me?" she asked.

"Who are you?"

"I am Tahoma," she said and smiled as she bowed briefly.

"What happened?" they asked her.

"I knew something wasn't right when you didn't show up to the mountain stream. I left Mai and Kai back there with the horses, and I headed into the forest, hoping to find you. My necklace started to glow bluer and bluer, and then I knew you were in danger."

"Your necklace?"

"Yes, I am Water Spirit. I have many gifts. One is my—well I guess you could say my amulet here. It glows to warn me. It sees the true nature of things, both good and bad. When it glows, I know someone is not as they appear to be."

"And it glowed bright blue from the thing in the forest?" Kokopelli asked, pointing in the direction of where the lurker had stood.

"Yes, exactly! Lurkers are ghostly entities—some good, some bad, all refusing to cross over into the spirit realm. The one that was following you appeared to be quite dangerous—lethal, I might think. It was a good thing I came along when I did. Have you seen this lurker before?"

Both the medicine man and Kokopelli shook their heads no.

"Hm," said Tahoma. "He could be following ... like your other trackers. You seem to have attracted a great deal of unwanted attention lately." She smirked. "Well, come." She motioned. "It's time to get back. I'll recount how I helped Mai as we walk. She's at the stream feeding Kai."

Kokopelli and the medicine man got up from the ground. The decomposing crawlers and insects were mysteriously already gone. They shuddered at the reminder of the crawling sensations at their feet, on their sandals, and on their legs. Tahoma had already turned and trekked ahead. They followed in single file.

Back at the mountain stream, Mai was taking care of Kai. She fed him, changed him, rocked him a little, and held him tightly. She smiled into his beautiful brown eyes, and he smiled right back. She was looking so closely into his eyes that she failed to notice them at first. The horses were at the stream and had not alerted her to their presence either. But suddenly, there they were ... beautiful, majestic elk. From what it looked like, a small herd of elk had come to the stream and were peacefully sipping water from the stream alongside the horses. She sat motionless with Kai. He moved his arms and legs a bit, but Mai's eyes were now on the elk. The leader of the elk herd came forward. He stood graceful and tall before her. He had a large rack of elk horns. He looked at her quietly and then looked at the baby. His eyes were a soft brown just like his coat. He blinked and then seemed to bow ever so slightly toward Mai and Kai. Then, just like that, he straightened. He turned and entered the forest. The other elk followed silently behind. One moment they were there, and the next moment the herd was drifting away into the deep forest.

Chapter Seven: Making an Ally

Sani was lying on the grass at the top of the hill. He looked carefully over the top and studied the settlement in the distance. He was weary from travel and had not eaten in two days. He had given the rest of the food in their pack to Mai and Kokopelli to keep up their strength, and he had gone without. He did not complain, though.

He watched the people moving within the settlement. It was a strange, foreign place in the valley below. The mountains with snowcapped peaks were closer now in range but still a long distance away. He saw men in strange clothing with pants and shirts and wide-brimmed hats that covered their heads. The women on the settlement looked even stranger, wearing long odd dresses that looked quite heavy and hot in the summer heat. The settlement had four-sided buildings with tall fronts and seemed to be made of wood or something. There were symbols on the fronts, symbols he could not read but he recognized from the map that Tsintah had given him. This was their writing he surmised, some way of identifying each building.

He looked to the river that they had been following closely in order to keep to the red line that Tsintah had made for them on the map. This place seemed to match the picture on the map where the river crossing was for humans. And there, before him was the river raft though it wasn't built like a canoe. It was rectangular in shape and quite large and he spent much time watching it ferry back and forth across the river. There were strange men on the river raft as well, pulling on ropes and using sticks to paddle through the water to head south and then north again.

The medicine man looked up at the hot sun beating down on them in the grass. Mai was also beside him lying on her stomach and looking in amazement and curiosity at the settlement. Sani looked behind them to the horses and to Kokopelli holding and feeding Kai near the river.

They had journeyed long and hard through the forests and yellow plains on this side of the river that was completely unfamiliar territory to the travel party. The medicine man remembered what he had been told about Spider Mother's warning. Those who travel past the Snake River are doomed to the destruction of the world. And yet here he was and here were the others. They were doing what Tsintah had told them they must do. And somewhere out here, in this wild new place, somewhere here was his father, Ahiga the Fire Spirit. Sani looked at the snowcapped mountain peaks and knew that was where they must go.

When they had left the mountain stream together, Tahoma had walked with them a short distance before bidding her goodbyes. She had turned to Mai and Kai at that point and looked at them in a protective mothering way as she had before at the mountain stream.

She slowly took off the amulet with crystal pendant, gently placed it in her hand, and closed her fingers around it. Then she looked at Mai purposefully and said, "Here, you need this more than I do." She opened her hand and gave the amulet to Mai. "Keep it close with you at all times. It will warn you when danger approaches. The pendant glows blue, depending on the level of danger—light blue to bright blue. When you see it glowing, the true nature of someone's character in your presence is revealed." She reached up to touch Mai's hair lightly and to place a strand of hair neatly behind Mai's ear. "Watch the pendant. I fear some of the people you may encounter on this journey will be not as they appear."

And that was all Tahoma said as she turned and walked away from them back into the forest.

They trekked for hours on end, taking several breaks, as the dire wolves would not be a threat for now. And so, they stopped periodically by the river to drink water, refresh the horses, and feed and change Kai. Mai and Kokopelli often played with Kai during these times. Their younger brother was proving to be a strong traveler as well. It helped that he was placed snug next to Mai, and they were grateful for the drinking pouch from Tsintah.

They stayed overnight amid the trees and just out of sight of the river. They dug the campfire deep into the ground so that it could not be seen by others. They took turns sleeping and keeping watch. Mai kept the amulet close in her satchel and took it out at night. She lay beside it with Kai and kept an eye on the crystal pendant. She was fearful of the dark entity that Kokopelli and the medicine man had encountered. They had told her of their experience, and she, in turn, spoke of seeing it out of the corner of her eye on their first journey on the horses into the forest.

"It appears we may have a follower. We'll have to stay closer to the river and out of the deep woods." Sani said, explaining the dark watchers to Mai. She shuddered.

They had traveled a total of three days. The food had run out by this time, and they were all hungry. Sani had fed the others first but now there was no food for any of them except Kai. They had the milk in the pouch but wanted to keep it for the baby, and so they had gone without food. The only weapon they had among themselves was a dagger. With no means to hunt or fish, they kept riding the horses or walking to reach the settlement that the medicine man had pointed out on the map. Sani also kept close in his satchel the odd-looking compass that Tsintah had given him, and he looked at it many times over to make sure they were headed the right way. They knew if they followed the river, they would eventually reach the river crossing settlement, and they had.

Sani quietly motioned to Kokopelli, and they crawled back from the hilltop. Then they headed back to the horses and Mai and Kai.

"We'll have to enter the settlement. There's no other way. We need food. We can't go much longer," said the medicine man.

The others nodded.

"We'll take the horses with us and the gear," Sani said as he reached into the pack and took the dagger. He lifted his tunic and placed the dagger so it was hidden under his tunic and tucked into the top of his britches.

"We walk from here," the medicine man directed. "We'll walk by the barge first and then turn and go into the settlement. These people are foreign here. I do not speak their language. Therefore, we will have to be very careful. Stay together and follow my lead. No sudden movements, and hold tight to the leashes of your horses. We will bargain with them somehow for food or beg if we must. And then we must continue our journey. There is much more to go. We have to head into those mountains, so I want you to be ready. I am sorry. This will get more difficult. For now, let's get some food and perhaps, if we are lucky, some shelter for the night. Be very careful now, and remember to follow my lead."

The travel party crested the hill together and began to walk toward the settlement. Outwardly, they appeared brave, but inwardly, each person questioned whether this was the right move and whether the settlement was safe.

They neared the barge dock. The usually bustling dock had grown quiet, as the people surrounding it were looking at the travel party cautiously. On either side of the dirt road, there were men and women who had stopped what they were doing to openly stare at them. The medicine man was ahead of the group. The others led the horses. But all of them felt immensely uncomfortable as they continued to walk and look around.

The barge master was barking orders for how to dock the raft. His helper, a young teen in long pants and a white shirt, had stopped docking the barge to look curiously at the travel party. He watched them with an intensity so much so that the raft crashed into the wood pier.

"Sam! Pay attention!" the barge master yelled. "Secure the

ropes now!"

Sam immediately snapped to attention and deftly went about his duties. But when the river raft was unloaded from travelers, he turned again to look at the other mysterious travelers who were now turning and walking up the main street of Stoney Creek.

"Ah no, ah no, no, no," Sam muttered to himself as he saw some of the boys like William Hun who had teased him unmercifully in school. He saw William and some others come out of the dry goods store and step onto the front porch to watch. They were laughing and pointing and staring unabashedly at the travelers with strange clothing and beautiful horses.

"Charles, I've got to go see what is going on. I'm sorry!" Sam said hurriedly, and he jumped onto the dock pier and headed swiftly through the crowd of folks and up the main road to follow the newcomers. These newcomers ... Sam knew there would be trouble, and yet, he went up the main road anyway. He tugged his wide-brimmed hat down and kept his face down as he walked near to the travel party now. He wanted not to be seen, but he needn't worry about that because all eyes were quietly and uncomfortably on the newcomers.

As the travel party and horses neared the dry goods store, young and arrogant William Hun stepped off the porch and walked nonchalantly over to Sani.

"Stop," he began. "What brings you here?"

But the medicine man kept walking because he did not understand the language of what was being said.

William Hun then placed his finger in Sani's chest. He spoke louder. "I said ... what brings you here?" And this time it really wasn't a question so much as a demand for an answer. William spit some tobacco chew onto the ground and looked back at the medicine man.

The medicine man looked at William. He was confused and said nothing. William looked over the travel party and Mai and Kai. Then he looked at the beautiful horses behind them. Those were some fine horses, and they seemed to be well handled because they followed easily behind the strangers. William reached for the horse leash in Mai's hand, and the medicine man subtly and imperceptibly moved his hand closer to his tunic where the dagger was hidden. Many of the crowd missed this subtle movement, but it was not missed by Sam Culvers, who was watching very carefully.

"Damn," he muttered. At that point, Sam knew he had no choice but to confront the situation.

Sam stepped from out of the crowd, placed his hat in his hand, and tried to appear apologetic to all.

"I'm sorry! I'm sorry!" he said, looking to everyone. "These are my guests." And he nodded to the travel party. He stepped forward so he could be clearly seen by the medicine man. Sani looked at him, and they locked eyes. Sam tried to smile at him, and the medicine man nodded at Sam. His hand also moved away from the dagger under his tunic.

William Hun looked mockingly and suspiciously at Sam Culvers. "Your guests?"

"Yes," said Sam, stammering for a moment. "My relatives." And he nodded and smiled at the medicine man, who, in turn, nodded and smiled back at the young man in front of him who looked familiar in appearance but spoke the other man's language.

A friend, thought the medicine man. *This is good. This is a blessing.*

William Hun would not let it go, though. He turned to the others in the crowd and laughed and looked incredulously at Sam Culvers again and mockingly said, "But, Sam, you don't have relatives. You're an orphan." And there was a touch of sneer in his voice.

"Sam's telling the truth," said a gravelly voice behind them.

Sam looked back, surprised to see the barge master standing not too far away watching everything. The barge master knew Sam was lying, but he covered for him anyways.

"These people are our guests tonight." He said in a matter-of-fact tone for all the crowd of gatherers on all the storefronts to hear. And just for added measure, the barge master moved aside his coat to reveal his revolver at his hip—just in case anyone wanted to challenge the barge master himself.

Sam looked gratefully for a second at Charles who stood stoically waiting. And one by one, the community members went about their normal daily activities ... the dry goods clerk to his counter, the travelers to the saloon, the preacher's wife to the church, and the school marm to the school. Only the travel party and their horses and Sam Culvers and Charles were left in the middle of the dirt road alone.

And then Sam said *hello* in his mother's native language to Sani, and the medicine man blinked and answered *friend* in return. They both smiled.

Chapter Eight: The Story of Sam

Sam Culvers had lived in Stoney Creek as far back as he could remember but had never felt a part of Stoney Creek. His mother and father came to the small southwestern Colorado town when he was six years old. At the time, the town had only seven or eight wood-planked structures. It was a small community, but even so, his family was never quite welcome there. They stayed on the outskirts of town, and Sam's father worked hard. His mother raised him in the little cabin near the river. He spent much of his time with her, and she taught him the old language. It was their secret communication to each other. He had been happy with his parents, but as life sometimes does, things took a turn for the worse after a while. Cholera had spread through the town due to the constant movement of travelers across the river barge to head into new pioneer territory. Both his mother and father became susceptible to the illness. First his mother passed, and then, in the short span of a few hours, his father passed too.

It was the barge master who found him. Charles' hulking figure stood in the doorway of the little cabin as the light filtered through. Sam had his back turned to the door and was sitting in a chair facing his parents' bed. Sam sat there silently. The bodies on the bed were still. It was the barge master who covered gently the faces of his parents with a blanket, took Sam's hand in his, and led him out of the little cabin that day.

In the days to come, Sam stayed with the barge master, who had been a neighbor to his parents. The barge master had seen his own heartache with the passing of his wife. Sam and the barge master attended the three funerals together in the graveyard to the northeast of town. They stood together as the preacher said a few words, and then they quietly walked back home together. On the day the little cabin was burned to the ground to prevent further spread of the cholera, it was barge master Charles who stood beside Sam again. As the flames overtook the building, Charles lightly placed his hand on Sam's shoulder. Nothing more was said. Nothing ever needed to be said much between those two.

When the little schoolhouse was finally completed on the north side of town, it was Charles who put Sam through school, walking him to school each morning before heading south to the barge for a long day's work. But things did not go well for Sam at the school. He did not fit in. He never seemed to fit in and was often bullied. He was a solitary boy much of the time. He went to school for three years before the barge master decided it was time to apprentice Sam and teach him the skills of barge traffic across the river.

Every day they rose before dawn to walk down to the docked barge. They worked in the sun, the heat, the wind, the rain, and the freezing cold. They worked year-round, every day until dusk. When they returned home together to the cabin, they often sat by the fire. Charles would fill his pipe and smoke in his rocking chair. It was Charles who taught Sam how to read and write better, as well as a little arithmetic. And at night by the fire, Charles liked for Sam to read to him. They often read what was available. They read from the old Bible a lot. When travelers came through on the barge, Charles often tried to negotiate with them for a good book or two ... for Sam. And it was by that firelight, that together they learned of the worlds of *Oliver Twist* and *Robinson Crusoe* and *Moby Dick*. They only had a few books and they read them repeatedly. Sometimes the stories would get so good that the usually stoic and hard-weathered old man would laugh or smile while smoking his pipe.

As the years grew on, the work continued on and on, and they fell into this same pattern of routine. When the church began to be built in town, the preacher stopped by the barge master several times to invite him and, if he wanted, the boy as well to be part of the congregation. Yet, they always declined.

The barge master never went to the little graveyard to the northeast near the new church. He never visited the tombstone of his deceased wife, but he kept a pocket watch with her black-and-white photo in his front pocket and would often look at it at night.

Sam Culvers, for his part, went to the graveyard a few times a year as he grew up into young manhood, but he was wary of the community, particularly the boys who had bullied him in school. Besides Charles, Sam mostly kept to himself, toiling relentlessly at the barge. He had become a muscular and fine young man of sixteen by the time the strangers arrived in the town of Stoney Creek—the strangers who would change everything about his life to come.

Chapter Nine: An Unlikely Guardian

The travel party stayed that night at the barge master's cabin. They tethered the horses outside on the railing, and the horses drank water and were refreshed at the trough. Meanwhile, the barge master had gone down to the dock and secured the barge. For the first day in many years, the barge was not running. He had placed a sign at the front that read: Closed Until Further Notice. The townspeople had looked at this skeptically. They gathered and gossiped throughout the evening on the front porches of the storefronts but mostly appeared to mind their own business and did not ask questions.

The barge master walked back to the cabin and helped with the placement of gear and getting the travelers settled in. He was uncomfortable with this arrangement, to say the least. But seeing the excitement in Sam's face and hearing it in his voice as he quietly talked in the other language to the others, he kept his opinions to himself. He was worried by the townspeople and warned Sam that the travelers would need to leave at dawn.

Sam quickly prepared a stew for the famished travelers, and they ate heartily while exchanging words in their native tongue, which Charles did not understand at all but Sam did. Charles noted that these travelers seemed to make Sam quite happy, and he had a sudden tug of resentment for them. They all ate dinner and cleaned up, and as dusk approached, Charles took the rifle from above the fireplace. The others stopped talking at this point and looked worriedly at Charles, but Sam reassured them.

Charles said nothing but went out onto the front porch with a chair and closed the front door to the cabin. He sat down on the hard, wooden chair and looked out onto Main Street. A few townspeople looked at him curiously and noted the rifle by his side. They said nothing, but Charles was certain words would be exchanged behind closed doors about the strangers who had entered their small western town. Charles wanted to make it abundantly clear to them that the strangers were under his protection, and so Charles sat on the porch, the rifle close by while he smoked his pipe and watched as the sun finally went down. Out of the corner of his eye, he watched young William Hun and his friends down the street to make sure they did not interfere again. Charles was worried about the magnificent horses the strangers had brought with them. He was concerned that if he did not stay out there and keep watch that night, these same horses might disappear come morning.

The door to the cabin entrance opened. Sam Culvers walked out and stood at the edge of the front porch. He did not look at Charles but said, "Why are you not inside with us?"

"Sam, I'm worried," said Charles, drawing slowly on his pipe. He nodded ever so slightly in the direction of William Hun and his crew.

Sam understood exactly what Charles was thinking. He said nothing, as was often their way, and yet he knew Charles better than anyone else here and trusted Charles.

"You didn't have to come to my rescue," said Sam softly. "I could have handled it myself."

And Charles, with his bulky, mammoth hands on his pipe, merely snorted. Then he said, "Yes, I suppose you could have. But just the same, I wanted to make sure."

Charles continued to smoke. Sam Culvers looked in the direction of William Hun and the others.

"I'm staying up tonight, and I'll watch the horses," Charles noted.

Sam nodded and turned to Charles. He looked at him directly but said nothing, and Charles looked at Sam and said nothing. Yet, they both understood.

Charles half smiled in the growing darkness at Sam. "When I took you in a long time ago, I knew that someday, someday you would need to head out on your own." He sighed deeply. "I know this place has never been your home."

And then there was silence.

Charles continued after drawing once more on his pipe. "There comes a time in a young man's life when he must set out on his own ... to set his own path through life."

Again, more silence.

"You're going with them, then?" Charles motioned to the closed entrance door to the cabin.

Sam looked at Charles sadly at this point and said, "Yes, they need my help."

Charles just nodded. He thought sadly to himself that there are some things which must be set free. He looked glumly down. He reached into his pocket and found the old watch and flipped it open. He looked at the old, faded black-and-white image of his deceased wife and nodded again. Then he said curtly, "Go inside, boy. Get your rest tonight. You will need it. I will be out here until just before dawn, and then I return to the barge. If I stay too long away from the barge, the townspeople ... you understand, right?"

"Yes," said Sam, and he headed back inside.

Charles flipped open the watch again. He pursed his lips ever so slightly, his jaw set firmly. He looked out onto the dark Main Street and kept watch over the horses.

Chapter Ten: Dream of Fire

Sam Culvers dreamed that night. He was standing in the dirt main road of Stoney Creek and looking across to the little cabin of his mother and father. It was catching ablaze just as it had done so many years ago. But this time, Sam was not a little boy. Sam was standing barefoot in the dirt. He had his long johns on. The fire was building intensely in the cabin, bursting through windows and the door. It spread onto the roof. The whole structure creaked and collapsed into itself. As he watched, the fire was spreading now. It was not just in the little cabin. The flames were showing up in the buildings to the left of the cabin. It was spreading down the street to each wooden-planked structure—the new church, the schoolhouse, the dry goods store ... Sam slowly turned to his left, watching as each building quickly caught fire ... even the saloon. He turned almost full circle until he was facing the river. In his dream, he had thought he was alone. But when he saw it, he began running in his long johns, his bare feet pounding the dirt to reach the water's edge. In the middle of the river, the barge was even ablaze. The flames were rising higher and higher, and in amidst the flames in the center stood a single, solitary figure.

Sam yelled, "Charles!" It was a long, drawn-out yell. The flames burst even higher across the barge, and in response, the man merely raised his right hand and slowly waved goodbye.

Sam woke up with a jolt. He was perspiring, and his eyes needed to adjust to the darkness of the cabin. He looked wide-eyed around and at the sleeping figures with blankets on the floor. Sam pushed back his blanket on his twin bed and rose quietly. He stepped over to the window that looked out onto the wood-plank front porch. He slightly moved the curtain to the right and saw the hulking silhouette of Charles sitting in the chair on the front porch. His rifle was still in his hands in front of him, but Charles did not move. Sam let go of the curtain, and it promptly fell back into place. He straightened up and looked at the others for a moment. Then he returned to bed, pulling the covers up. He shifted onto his side so he could face the familiar planks of the cabin wall. He looked at them for a while and then eventually drifted off to sleep.

In the morning, before dawn, the travel party was assembling their gear and gathering the horses. Kai was again wrapped snugly with Mai. Charles stood on the front porch in front of the hard chair he had sat in all night. His rifle was now beside the chair and propped up on the wall. The roof overhang cast a shadow upon his weary face. Sam walked out the front door to the cabin and stood in front of Charles. He had something in his hands that he presented then to Charles: his worn-out dog-eared Bible. Charles took the gift and looked grimly down at it before looking back into Sam's eyes. They shared a moment.

Charles squinted his eyes ever so slightly, as if to hold back something, and his lips were firmly pursed. His jaw was set stoically. He looked directly at Sam who looked up at him with a half-smile. Sam nodded briefly and then put on his wide-brimmed hat. He turned to go, but he stopped when he felt Charles's left hand come to rest lightly on his shoulder—come to rest the same way it had gently so many years ago when he stood as a child before his parents' cabin. Sam looked again at Charles. Charles looked down momentarily and then pursed his lips again and nodded his reassurance to Sam that it was okay to go now. Charles then reached over, picked up the rifle, and handed it to Sam.

"For your protection. There are two rounds in it. Be safe, Sam."

Sam stepped off the front porch and onto the dirt street of Stoney Creek. He did not bother to look around much as the travel party and horses slowly made their trek through town and to the north. But he did look briefly to the right as they passed the graveyard and looked at the two tombstones off to the side. The travel party kept walking quietly except for a low neigh or two from the horses.

Charles watched them go from the front porch. He still held the old Bible in his right hand. He turned to enter the cabin and placed the Bible on his bed. He grabbed his wide-brimmed hat from the hook by the door and softly closed the entrance door to the cabin. Once again, he stood on the front porch and this time looked left toward the river to the docked barge. He put on and adjusted his hat and then stepped off the porch and turned toward the river, slowly walking alone to the barge.

Chapter Eleven: The Tracker

Neqael could shift into a Smilodon, a saber-toothed tiger, a remnant of the third world. This dangerous shape-shifter had grown disinterested in the trivialities of men several hundred years ago. Their comings and goings, their births and deaths mattered very little to him—specks of dust in the world. Except this one group of humans mattered—or at least mattered for the present moment to his leader, Hashkeh Naabah.

Some commoners—poor, dirty commoners—actually mattered to the Haeynodon shape-shifter. They had escaped fate quite unexpectedly. These humans of little distinction had escaped the dire wolf party and Hashkeh Naabah himself. They had snatched the baby and run. They had disrupted the order of carefully crafted plans to come. This angered Hashkeh Naabah, who demanded their return.

"It does not matter really what happens to the others," said the leader in their private meeting after the council. "Bring the child back. Dispatch of the others or bring them back. Your choice."

So Neqael was sent like a bounty hunter to fetch the baby quietly, while Hashkeh Naabah seethed with wounded pride. The dire wolf pack was already on their trail. Sending the Smilodon hunter as well was just an extra precaution, the Hyaenodon leader reasoned.

The humans were proving to not be easy to track. If the Smilodon was capable of emotion, he would express frustration and possibly even pity for these humans. Yet the Smilodon was one of the twenty, the shape-shifter council, and that honor had not come through weakness of character. The Smilodon already knew he would not bring the others back, just the baby.

All the creatures could do was run. Eventually, he would corner them.

Neqael moved swiftly through shadow and moonlight. His great prowess was well known among the decayers. He was cunning and clever. He was also unmerciful. His razor-sharp saber teeth gleamed in the light of the midsummer moon. He stealthily moved across the forest. He remembered the cliff dwellers and how he had sometimes watched them covertly, listening to the sound of human civilization—a utensil banging against pottery, voices, laughter, a baby crying. The moon continued to shine in a waning crescent over the forest.

He remembered how one night he had paused briefly in the light of an opened entryway, having slipped stealthily past the sentries to the village. The Smilodon mused at how vulnerable the humans always made themselves. He remembered seeing a woman tending to her child's bed. She straightened. Their eyes met briefly. It was a short exchange, and the big cat was gone. He remembered how that night he had passed a drunkard in the dirt-trodden maze of streets in the cliff village. The man lay half inebriated against an earthen wall. Unbeknownst to the man, their destinies intertwined that night. The human had smiled drunkenly at the looming, ominous Neqael. He innocently reached out his fingers to touch the fur façade of an eons-old demon cat. The Smilodon, bemused, had spared him perhaps on a whim. That was many moons ago—moonlit nights like this one.

Neqael moved through the thick, green undergrowth with relative ease. He had not traveled this far east before. He was searching this night because Hashkeh Naabah requested a favor, and no one, not even a demon cat, denied his request without fear of the consequences.

Eventually, the saber-toothed tiger came to the water's edge—a wide river. He followed the tracks to the cliff and looked over, surveying the wreckage below the waterfall cliff. He looked beyond to the other embankment. This was problematic. He prowled back and forth and thought carefully. He would figure a way to cross, and cross he would. Neqael quietly looked into the dark night.

It was just a matter of time before he would find them.

Chapter Twelve: A Shocking Discovery

With Sam's help, the travel party was making its way northeast along the red path provided by Tsintah. Sam explained as best he could the wording of the map to Sani as they journeyed by foot. Together, they talked of this unfamiliar territory. They walked for a long distance and then rode the horses. They rested several times throughout that day. The midsummer heat and sun were bearing down on them, and at times throughout the journey, Sam let the others borrow his wide-brimmed hat, which they found quite amusing and enjoyed immensely. The day had proven to be a good one for the travel party thus far. They had food in their packs, they were well rested from the night prior, and they seemed to make progress toward the second mark on the red path. From what they could tell from the map, the burned smudge identified a spot just to the southeast of a major town called Silver Springs, and the image there showed a rock house of some kind.

It was in the late afternoon. They happened upon the railroad tracks of the Silver Springs Railroad. They had entered a canyon and were winding through it when they came across a giant structure of wood and metal that spanned across the two sides of the canyon gorge. They quietly crossed under the bridge, as Sam had identified it, and they were coming out of the canyon when they stopped to look back and take a break. What they saw behind them surprised them.

Sam had said earlier the railroad was being constructed. "Notice those wood boards. Those are called railroad ties. The hard metal that flows north and south of us on the ties is called the track. The train travels on these tracks." He pointed to the construction work. The others had never seen a rail train, and so this was a great mystery to them.

"Why build this?" said Kokopelli, looking at the mess of

construction, blown-away rocks, and felled trees. Further on down from the canyon, there seemed to be some type of railway station house. Beside it, to their horror, sat a large stack of sun-bleached animal bones. Beside the stack was another that was just as large of what appeared to be animal furs.

"What?" Sani said in shock.

Sam looked to the bison head bones and the bison furs sitting in the sun. "Buffalo," he said quietly to the medicine man.

"Many buffalo," said Sani. "Why do they need so much?"

"They sell them," said Sam. "They sell the bones and the hides. There are men who are famous for this, like Buffalo Bill. They ride with the railroads and kill the herds for meat for the workers. They leave the bones and hides here to dry and then transport them."

"Where do they go?" asked Mai sadly.

Sam motioned his hand farther east. "To other towns and places called cities. I have never been to a city, but I learned of them in the newspapers I would read to Charles. I read about Chicago. I would like to see this place Chicago someday."

"I do not want to see this place you speak of," said Kokopelli harshly, "if they do this." He nodded his head to the sun-bleached bones. "There is no need for so many buffalo skins."

They decided at that point to continue onward and not stop there. They could hear the sounds of steel on steel further down the line and shouts of men from time to time.

"Railroad workers," explained Sam again. "Building the line to Silver Springs."

"Ah, Silver Springs. The place on the map near where we must go," said the medicine man.

"Yes," said Sam.

They started to head north and northeast a bit, keeping along the railway lines but just out of view skirting the trees. They camped overnight again amid the trees, careful to hide their fire from the railroad workers to the west.

On the second day in the morning, they noted the railroad spanned over some gentle cascades of water. They needed water for themselves and for the horses. So carefully and slowly, they journeyed back to the west to the cascades and let the horses drink and rest while they ate some and cared for the baby. They were near the cascades when they heard the sound of the steam locomotive moving. It came from the north and seemed at first to be moving slowly but then was suddenly upon them. Overhead, it thundered over the rails, belching steam and smoke, its steel wheels turning swiftly. It was big and black, and when it crossed over them, the horses bucked and neighed in fright, and everyone but Sam hit the dirt to crouch low in shock. *What is that monstrous thing?* they thought to themselves. It was their first encounter ever with a train locomotive. The locomotive passed them and whistled loudly as it rapidly headed south.

They quickly left the cascades. They did not care much for this outside world, and Sam seemed apologetic and silent about the experience. They returned to the woods and followed the compass northeast. Another night fell, and in the morning, they rose, checking their supplies and discovering that yes, they would need food again. Sam had Charles's rifle and knew how to fire it, but he only had two rounds with him. He had not attempted to go hunting yet. Besides, they were nearing the spot on the map. As they neared it, they grew quieter and quieter. Tsintah had said that this test would be harder than the last, and none of them were looking forward to what they might encounter.

They saw the rock structure in the hills heading up into the mountains. It was in a cleared space of land and sat under a steep ridge of tall and thick coniferous trees. They noted that the trees were changing here, and Sam had explained that it was due to the mountain elevations rising higher.

It was a square and quite large all rock house with four side walls. It appeared to have lights on inside, as they could see from several windows. They watched the house first, studying the goings on around it. There was a red barn to the north of the house, an outhouse, and a well pump. There was also a sign near the trail leading to the house. A man and woman worked outside the house tending things.

The woman wore a long yellow dress and apron and appeared to be doing laundry outside at a bucket and washboard at the pump and hanging the clean clothes on a line. The man was working in the garden to the right of the red barn. He was pulling vegetation from the garden. A young teenage girl, quite lovely actually, had begun to walk down the path leading to the sign for the main road. She had long brunette hair, and she waited by the sign. It appeared she was waiting for visitors from the Silver Springs area along the road from the north. She sat down on a rock near the sign and sat there for a while playing with the ribbons of her pretty bonnet.

They did not seem threatening to the travel party. They did not seem threatening at all. And yet, Mai's amulet necklace and crystal pendant around her neck had begun to glow a very dark blue. Kokopelli, Sani, and Sam also looked at the pendant. They retreated farther into the woods to consult. They decided to stay back from the rock house that night. Mai and the medicine man and Kai would encamp with the horses. Meanwhile, Kokopelli and Sam were designated to be lookout scouts for the goings-on at the rock house. The medicine man built a low fire again at the encampment. They were growing hungry again, but they would wait—wait until they found out what Kokopelli and Sam would discover that night.

Kokopelli and Sam ventured forth quietly through the foliage of the forest. They watched the house from a distance, noticing the kerosene lights through the windows. The pretty brunette girl was no longer by the sign. She seemed to be inside the house with the older man and woman. They also seemed to have visitors, for there was an odd-shaped vehicle up the drive.

Sam whispered to Kokopelli, "That is called a wagon. They travel on those with two horses hitched to it. The horses must be in the red barn resting. I am going up there while they are inside. I want to read that sign so we know what this place is. I'll be right back. If anything happens, head back to the others."

Sam cautiously darted through the forest and inched his way up to the sign. He had to get quite close in order to read it in the darkness. As he was reading, a door to the rock house opened and slammed shut. Kokopelli looked worriedly at Sam, but Sam had already crouched and headed back over the main road and down into the ditch. He seemed to be lying very low in the ditch.

The man had come out of the house. He was quickly followed by the older woman. They seemed to be arguing about something but doing it quietly outside. Sam watched them curiously. The woman smoothed her hair and apron and went calmly back inside with a smile. The man headed to the red barn scowling.

He opened the door to the red barn and brought a horse out into the moonlight. He seemed to be checking the saddle pouches on the horse. He also checked inside the wagon, and Sam surmised that the horse and wagon did not belong to the man. In fact, the sign on the road had said that this place was an inn. It was a place for travelers on the main road to stop, have dinner, and rest for the night. And here, this man was searching the pouches of one of the travelers' horses. That put Sam on his guard immediately, and he lay as low as he could on the surface of the grass in the ditch, no longer watching what the man was doing. But he listened, and in a few short moments, he heard the door to the inn open and shut again. He cautiously looked up, and the red barn was closed. Sam crawled backward until he reached the cover of the woods and returned to Kokopelli. He communicated what he saw to Kokopelli, and together, they looked suspiciously at the house, concerned for the traveler or travelers within that night.

They couldn't see what was going on inside the house. They had no other choice but to brave the possibility of getting caught. They would have to move in to see what was going on. On the right side of the house were a couple of thick bushes and trees. So, in the moonlight, they crossed the main road to the right and climbed up the embankment and then moved swiftly toward the bushes beneath and beside one of the windows. When they had both reached the window and crouched down, it was decided between them with head nods that Sam should be the one to look. And slowly, he raised his head above the bush just a little.

He could see the house was nicely furnished, and the inhabitants were sitting at a large kitchen table having dinner. The older man and woman sat beside each other. The young girl sat near the traveler. He appeared to be a young man, and he was alone. He was smiling at the brunette who seemed to be flirtatious. As they ate at the dinner table, Sam noticed that the brunette was coyly playing footsie under the table with the young man. She smiled at him, and he seemed to blush. The older man and woman appeared not to notice this. Sam wondered why they did not notice.

They finished dinner, and the women set to work on cleaning up, while the men turned toward the living room area. Sam quickly ducked back down, worried for a moment that he had been caught and they would have to make a sudden dash down the embankment and into the woods. He worried the older man might have a rifle too. But he waited and realized that they had not seen him peering through the window. He put his finger to his lips and then whispered to Kokopelli what he had seen.

Sam decided to brave a window glance again. He raised his head again ever so slightly. The men were sitting on chairs in the living room. They were smoking and engaging in friendly banter. The women finished in the kitchen. The young woman began to head to the living room smiling, but the older woman grabbed her arm tightly. There was a quick exchange between the two women, and then the older woman released her. The girl headed into the living room. She smiled flirtatiously at the man and sat quite boldly near him on the settee. He smiled at her again. It was clear that he was trying to hold a discussion with the older man and woman but was distracted by the beauty of the young girl from time to time in the conversation.

The group sat in the living room for a while, and then the young man seemed to stand up and excuse himself. The older woman got up and turned to walk toward Sam's window. Sam fell abruptly to the dirt and pulled Kokopelli with him. They froze. They waited. The woman had seemed to pick up the kerosene lamp by the side table by the window and must have walked away with it because the light retreated away from the window. Soon, all the lights in the first floor were out, and Sam and Kokopelli noted that the people inside must have gone upstairs to rest. Kokopelli and Sam looked up at the second-story lights. They motioned to each other to retreat over the embankment and down it. As they were going, they heard a window sill being opened from above. They got down into the grass again and lay very still. Nothing happened, so they hurried low and crouching over the main road, into the ditch, and behind a bush. There they sat again and watched.

The window that had opened was the window to the bedroom directly above where they had crouched previously. The lights were on in the second floor, and they could see into the bedroom. The older woman was showing the man his room, and she had opened the window for him. The white curtains were billowing softly out the window. On this side of the house but toward the back appeared to be the girl's room, and Sam guessed that the older couple slept on the other side of the house. There appeared to be three rooms upstairs.

The front door to the house opened and shut again, and the

old man was heading toward the outhouse. He stayed for a while and then returned to the main house. Before long, all the lights in the house had gone out. Sam and Kokopelli were continuing to watch and wondering if they should return to the encampment when they heard a loud screech owl scream from the large oak tree near the opened window. Kokopelli was immediately on his guard. He knew that owls were bad omens, and screech owls in particular boded not well for those they encountered. He suddenly did not want to stay to watch the others anymore. He did not trust this place. He did not trust that owl, and he watched the opened window of the young man's bedroom with great concern.

An hour had gone by. They could hear the howling of coyotes nearby in the night. The stars had come out as well. They were getting uncomfortable in their crouched position. And then, they saw it. The screech owl screamed once more.

The window sill to the young girl's room was suddenly forced open about halfway. Fingers were at the base of the window and pushing it up ... but they were not like normal fingers. Both Kokopelli and Sam looked at each other in alarm. The fingers were red and seemed more like claws, long and frightening. The hands disappeared into the dark room, and for a moment, all they saw was the billowing of the curtains. Then something began to crawl out of the window, and it definitely was not human. It was red and meaty, as if it had no flesh—just beady eyes and no hair. It crawled out of the window and along the wall toward the young man's window. It had sharp claws for hands as well, and it scaled the walls effortlessly as if it could even fly. For a brief second, it was out in the open, and then suddenly, it had crawled into the darkened room of the young man.

Kokopelli and Sam looked again at each other. Kokopelli began to move out from behind the bush toward the house.

Sam grasped Kokopelli's arm and sadly shook his head. "No, it's too late."

And he was right. Whatever the creature was, it was in

the bedroom now, and they heard muffled noise and then a startled cry. Kokopelli and Sam just looked at each other, their eyes wide open. Sam grasped Kokopelli's arm tightly. *Wait.* He seemed to say. *Wait.*

They looked sadly at the upper floor window when a light had come on. They ducked down behind the bush. It was the older woman in her pajamas holding the kerosene lamp. The woman was standing at the doorway. They could barely see the bed from the light. They could see the man's body on the bed, and the creature they surmised had once been the beautiful brunette he flirted with was sitting on his chest, appearing to suck his breath or his energy or something from his mouth. It was a hideous, frightening red beast of a thing. It looked like some kind of succubus hag.

The older woman just stood in the doorway. She smiled and placed the kerosene lamp on the dresser. She took off her pajamas, and they dropped to the floor. Kokopelli and Sam could no longer look away. They couldn't tear their eyes away from what was happening. Next, the old woman seemed to peel off her own skin as if it were like her pajamas and then dropped the skin to the floor. She resembled the hideous monster on the bed feeding on the young man's energy. The older woman creature moved toward the bed too now. The man was not moving, and as she got closer and closer, both Kokopelli and Sam shut their eyes and averted their glances. There were no more sounds from the young traveler.

"Witches," muttered Kokopelli, now knowing what evil he was facing. "Cursed witches. Hags."

They remained there the rest of the night behind the bush. They had gone through a great deal of shock, and both young men were shaking a bit, though they did not tell each other. As the moon shifted lower on the horizon, they saw what looked like the skin of the young man thrown halfway out the window, hung over the sill as if to dry. They wondered what happened to the rest of the young man, and soon they saw the older man emerge from the house carrying the large metal tub to the pump—the same tub that had been used for the laundry earlier in the day. The older man took things from the tub, set them on the rock wall beside the pump, and began hacking at them with a cleaver.

Suddenly, the young men knew exactly what had happened to the traveler and what would probably be served for dinner tomorrow to the next group of unsuspecting travelers. They could not stay there any longer. Their stomachs churned and lurched, and they both shook with fear. The old man continued to hack at the meat on the rock wall, the skin continued to dry on the window ledge, and Sam and Kokopelli retreated very quietly back into the woods. When they hit a distance where they were certain they could not possibly be heard, they looked at each other and ran back to the encampment. When they reached the travel party, the medicine man was standing there waiting for them. He was looking at them inquisitively and searching for answers. Mai and Kai were asleep. Mai was clutching the amulet in her hand. It still shone a dark blue in the dark. The horses were nearby. Izou was asleep, curled up in the grass. And suddenly, Kokopelli bent over and heaved onto the ground.

Chapter Thirteen: Don't Stay at the Inn

In the dark of the early morning, gathered around the fire, the young men and the medicine man sat. They did not wake Mai and Kai. They let them rest. Kokopelli and Sam sat close to each other cross-legged and looked into the fire. They seemed visibly shaken to Sani, who sat quietly waiting for them to speak. The fire crackled. The light of the amulet shown dark blue, and when a coyote howled in the distance, Kokopelli moved, suddenly startled. Sam remained stoic, looking into the fire and began to tell the medicine man the story of all they had seen. He did not leave anything out. He told it all, and when he was done, he looked into Sani's eyes over the fire.

There was only silence at first, and then the medicine man nodded.

"Boo hags," he said slowly and low in their native tongue. He also looked into the fire grimly. No one spoke. And then the medicine man began to speak again. "They consume the life force of their victims. They eat their energy through their mouths as they sleep. If the victim wakes up while they attack, they also steal the skin. We will need to formulate a plan. They are cunning and full of deceit ... dangerous, very dangerous." He stoked the fire.

He got up and reached for the pack and began to place what weapons they had on the dirt ground: the dagger and the rifle with two rounds—that was all. He grabbed the last remaining bread from Stoney Creek and offered it to both young men. Neither Kokopelli nor Sam could eat.

"You must gather your strength." He motioned for them to take the bread again. Again, they refused. They looked around at the darkness and up at the starlight night.

And then together, over the fire that early morning, the three of them prepared their plan. When they had finished talking, Sani looked at Sam pointedly. "You will be the one to go into the house. It is the only way. You are the only one who speaks their language."

Sam breathed in deep and pursed his lips. He set his jaw with resolve as he had seen Charles do so many times in the past and said, "Yes."

"You will know when they are near when you encounter three things. What you heard tonight, the screeching of the owl ... that is a warning of their presence. Owls live and reside near dark creatures. Second, when you are in the room lying on the bed, you will feel that the room gets warm and damp—another indicator. Lastly"—and he looked at both of the young men—"you will know a boo hag is near by the smell of rotting flesh."

Sam swallowed a thick lump in his throat. His eyes were wider, but he remained stoic and resolute. "Yes," was all he said.

The medicine man looked at the dagger. He picked it up, turning it in his hand. "We will use this to sharpen some sticks, turn them into makeshift spears. That is all we have between the three of us. That ... and my fire abilities."

They did not speak much more than that. The sun would be rising soon. They did not think it was a good idea to awaken Mai and the baby.

"It will have to be the three of us. Mai and the baby and the horses must stay here. You will ride in on a horse from the north road, appearing as a traveler," Sani said to Sam. "Do as they say. Let them invite you into the house, but do not take the dinner. Excuse yourself early at a little after dusk to retire to the bedroom. You must lie on the bed and pretend you are asleep. Allow them to open the bedroom window. And you must take this with you." He then took the dagger and handed it handle first to Sam.

Sam accepted it with a slow sad nod.

"Okay," said Sani, looking down. "Sam?"

"Yes," said Sam.

"This morning at first light, you will teach Kokopelli how to handle the rifle. Go over this with him many times—how to point it, how to use it, how to use these things you call rounds."

The medicine man then looked directly at Kokopelli in the dark. "Kokopelli, you will only have two chances—two shots to kill the boo hag who crawls out the window." He stoked the fire and then looked directly at Kokopelli so that the full effect of his next words would set in. "Kokopelli, you must not miss. Do you understand?"

"Yes," said Kokopelli, and he felt the stomach sickness in his belly again.

"Okay, we have only a short time before daylight. Rest, you both. You will need your strength ... and your resolve. I will keep watch over the night."

And the two young men lay down on the dirt and grass. They attempted to sleep, but neither one really could. Instead, they looked at the woods and the fire. Only Mai and Kai slept soundly during those last few hours before dawn.

At dawn, Mai and Kai arose, and Mai fed Kai and held him. Izou crawled in and out of the packs searching for food and then settled into the grass to nibble on leaves, having found nothing else to eat. They all shared the last swigs of the water container. Most of the food was gone. Mai ate some. Kokopelli and Sam had lost their appetites. The medicine man refused to eat their last portions and so placed them in the pack carefully wrapped up. The horses were surely getting thirsty themselves, but they had nearby grass to eat.

Sam showed Kokopelli the rifle. Kokopelli listened intently to Sam's every word. Sam carefully took the two rounds out of the rifle and then showed Kokopelli the rifle and how to use it. He explained everything he could about the rifle to Kokopelli, and Kokopelli just nodded with wide eyes. He warned Kokopelli that there might be a kickback when it fired, and he explained what to do if he should lose his stance or fall down. Throughout the morning, they went over the rifle repeatedly, as if their very lives depended on it, for surely they did.

The travel party sat around the fire the remainder of the morning and into the afternoon. They spoke very little, and the comradery that they had before was now gone. No more smiles. No more laughter. Izou continued to move about the grass, but sensing the atmosphere of the party, he too stayed close to Kokopelli throughout the afternoon. Meanwhile, Mai and Sam took care of Kai. She knew something had gone terribly wrong the night before, but the others refused to speak of it. The medicine man had warned her to keep Kai as happy as possible that day, and if he should cry at any moment, to rock him gently. Sani also explained to her that the three of them would set out that night for the main road, and it was very important that she and Izou and Kai remain at the encampment and wait for them. They would secure Izou in a satchel before they left. She must keep the fire going and keep Kai very quiet. The medicine man also warned that if anything should happen to them, Mai should take the horses, as well as the compass, map, and gear and return southwest to the cliff village.

"Don't go looking for us no matter what. Understood?"

"Yes," she said.

And with that, Mai also fell silent that afternoon. When it began to near sunset, the three men set out from the encampment toward the main road. Sam took a horse. He positioned his hat carefully on his head, straightened up his clothes as best he could to look like an ordinary traveler on the road, and placed the dagger in a secret place, hidden in the waistband of his trousers. They traveled for a distance silently together. And then as they neared the rock house looming in the distance, they turned to each other and clasped each other's arms in solidarity.

Sam got onto the horse and rode off. He skirted around the rock house out of view and traveled some distance north until he could turn east and get on to the main road. He positioned the horse in the center of the road, and it began to saunter down the road. He straightened his back and rode forward, down the hill toward the rock house inn. The adrenaline was already rushing through his veins. Though he did not show it, he was frightened. The horse sensed his fear and neighed some and seemed to resist moving down the hill. But he gently kicked his leg into the horse's side, and together, they ambled down the road.

Kokopelli and Sani positioned themselves in the woods just out of view to watch. The medicine man held two makeshift spears from wood he had found in the forest. The points were super sharp. Kokopelli held the loaded rifle in his hands possessively and gingerly. He was fully aware that the most important part of the plan was in his hands.

They watched the rock house. They had been watching the rock house for a while, and nothing appeared out of the ordinary. The old woman was again wearing the yellow dress and apron and appearing to wash clothes in the bucket. The old man was tending to vegetation in the garden again. The old woman was using the pump and the washboard and hanging clothes on the line. The lights were again on in the rock house. Meanwhile, down the path, the other boo hag was sitting on the rock and waiting at the inn sign. Except this time, it was not the beautiful brunette girl they had seen earlier. This time, they were looking at the visage and appearance of the young male traveler from the night before. The boo hag was wearing his skin and his clothes too. They also noticed that there was no longer a sign of the wagon from the night before. It had simply vanished, presumably into the red barn.

Kokopelli stared aghast at the boo hag in the young man's skin. It was casually sitting on the rock as if it did not have a care in the world and smiled and got up from the rock when it saw the lone rider on the road up the hill. It whistled back to the old man and old woman, and they noted the whistle but otherwise appeared to go about their work as usual.

The boo hag straightened its clothes, smiled broadly, and waved at the stranger sauntering down the hill. The stranger was Sam. Kokopelli watched him ride straight-backed up to the boo hag. If Sam had noticed the change and appearance of the boo hag, he did nothing to show it. Kokopelli felt sick to his stomach as he watched from the woods.

He and the medicine man could not see or hear what happened next between Sam and the other young man. Sam stopped his horse in the road, and the two discoursed for a while. Then Sam moved his horse casually up into the driveway of the old rock house and up the beaten path. The boo hag followed beside Sam's horse, smiling and seeming to laugh. The old man in the garden looked up from weeding and then stepped out of the garden to greet and welcome Sam. The old woman also stood up from behind the wash tub, brushed off her apron, and appeared courteous and kind to Sam. There was an exchange. Dusk was arriving. They welcomed Sam to their house, and Sam got off the horse and handed the reins over to the old man. He took off his hat and held it in his hands, being a gentleman for the lady, and he smiled, but when they turned to go into the house, Sam looked very briefly into the woods for Kokopelli and Sani.

Sam went into the house and made the usual pleasantries as a guest. The old woman smiled at him and offered to take his hat. He obliged, and she placed it on a hook near the entryway.

Sam walked into the kitchen where the table was set for a nice meal. He could smell the meat cooking on the stove, and he swallowed a hard lump in his throat. He cleared his throat and said to the others, "Why, thank you! You are some gracious hosts. I would love to have dinner with you tonight. It smells delicious, but I have already eaten in Silver Springs and am quite full."

He watched the brief exchange among the three. They seemed to accept his excuse, though. He kept his eyes on them and smiled. "I would, however, love a nice smoke in your beautiful living room. Perhaps some good conversation, and then I must retire early for bed. I am to be headed out very early in the morning on my journey and am quite tired already."

"Where do you come from, sir, and what is your name?" the old woman asked. She seemed to be sizing him up, and perhaps it was just Sam's imagination, but she seemed to be carefully looking him over.

Sam was trying hard to remain stoic, and he thought to himself, *Be like Charles. Be like Charles. Don't lose your cool. Be like Charles.*

He smiled. "I come from a place yonder from here up north called Westcliffe. It's a beautiful place to live, surrounded by the mountains. You would love it there. My name is Sam."

"Sam," said the young man softly. The name seemed to draw slow on the man's tongue, as if it would slither.

"Yes, sir." Sam nodded.

"And what brings you south, Sam?" asked the old man. He motioned to Sam and then to the living room and offered him the settee while he sat across in the rocking chair. The old woman tended to things in the kitchen. Sam had his back to her and was acutely aware of the dagger at his waist. He sat down on the couch, and the young man promptly sat on the other side of the settee. There was no flirting with the stranger this time, no playfulness.

No playing with one's food, Sam thought to himself uncomfortably. He wanted to move farther away from the young man who smiled at him, but instead, he calmed himself. Inside, Sam was deeply horrified by the boo hag choosing to wear the young traveler's skin like a new outfit. But outwardly, he showed no visible signs of stress.

The old man offered to share a smoke or two with Sam, and they engaged in some banter—some small talk and pleasantries about the weather, about mining, the railroads, gardening, and such. When the old man began to query him repeatedly about Westcliffe, a place Sam had read about in a newspaper but never actually seen himself, Sam had to come up with some whoppers to keep them happy. The old woman finished in the kitchen and came over to sit as well. Sam was sweating by this point and had to swallow a lump in his throat repeatedly. At one point, he stammered. He was acutely aware that the young man—or rather, boo hag—was staring at him. He did his best to be at ease. *Be like Charles*. He kept saying this over and over in his head. He didn't want to be here. He wanted to be back on the barge with the barge master, back in Stoney Creek. He was beginning to feel deeply afraid.

Eventually, the conversation met a lull. It was getting dark outside the windows, and so Sam stood up and excused himself to retire early to bed. The three others in the room looked pointedly at each other and also seemed to be relieved that the conversation was over. The old woman got up and picked up the kerosene lamp from the side table by the window and then led the way up the narrow staircase. Sam followed, and behind him, trailed the young man and old man. Sam swallowed hard again. At the top of the stairs, the old woman turned right and went down a narrow corridor to his room. She opened the door and kindly welcomed him in.

She motioned to the bed and set the kerosene lamp on the dresser beside the door. Sam looked down at the door as well and noted the door lock seemed jammed. He also noted that the old man and young man had retired to their rooms without offering a good night. They had closed their doors behind them, and he could see the light from the cracks under their doors. He swallowed again. He was sweating profusely now. The old woman was explaining to him that the room could get very hot in this midsummer, so she walked to the window on the opposite wall and opened it up halfway just as Sam had seen her do the night before. He looked at the bed with pillows and headrest. It was a full-size bed and would have seemed quite nice if he had not thought of what happened to the last occupant of the bed. The old woman watched him and smiled again. He smiled back and said, "Thank you."

She said, "Well, if there is anything further you need, please do not hesitate. Please, Sam, get some rest and have a pleasant stay with us." She smiled once more.

Sam felt a sickening dread. "Yes, I do believe I shall," was all he said.

And with that, she crossed to the entryway and shut the door behind her. Sam let out a deep breath. He did not like standing with his back to the door or near the open window, so he stood at the foot of the bed. He took off his shoes, trousers, and shirt, leaving his socks, underpants, and undershirt on with the dagger tucked securely into his underpants. He blew out the kerosene lamp and lay down on the bed as if to sleep. And he lay there for a while, sweating, his heart pounding, his every nerve tensed and ready for an attack, listening to every creak and every little noise inside and outside the house.

It was after about two hours of lying there that he heard it. He could not see well in the room. It was quite dark, but by the moonlight of the window and the billowing curtains, he heard the screech owl again in the large oak tree. The scream was, to him, bloodcurdling, and he began to shake. The room was getting hotter, it seemed. He continued to lie on the bed.

Meanwhile, Sani and Kokopelli had moved carefully out of the woods and positioned themselves as planned. The medicine man was to the corner of the front entrance squatted down low and holding the makeshift spears in either hand tightly. Kokopelli was standing in the shadows of the large oak tree where he had a good vantage point to see the boo hag's window open. He was just enough in the shadows that he hoped the boo hag would not see him first ... and it didn't.

The boo hag quietly opened the second upstairs window. The window raised halfway, and just as before, the curtains billowed in the night. Kokopelli could not see into the darkness of the room, but he knew that in a matter of moments, he must fire the rifle and must not miss. He held the rifle tightly and began to slowly bring it up to aim as Sam had shown him. He prepared to move out into the moonlight when the time came. Sam had warned him, "You only got two rounds. You must get within close range and fire quickly."

The boo hag, all red and skinless and bald and terrifying with claws for hands, moved out of the window and began to crawl across the rock wall toward the other open window. Kokopelli stepped quietly forward one step, then two steps. The rifle was raised; he just had to aim and pull the trigger. He hoped he did not miss. The boo hag crawled sideways across the rock wall, now only inches from the other open window where Sam lay. Kokopelli moved forward one more step and then one step farther, when—snap. A twig under his foot broke in half.

The boo hag swiveled its head and looked right at him. It screamed then, a sound like the screech owl, and Kokopelli aimed and fired. The shot resounded in the night and threw him backward. He was not ready for it.

It appeared he had hit the boo hag. Lucky shot. The hag screeched again and then fell to the ground below. Kokopelli got up quickly with the rifle and then moved as close as he could within feet of the hag. The hag was curled inward from the wound that had torn through its back and abdomen, but it was still alive. Kokopelli aimed carefully and close and fired once more.

At the sound of the first gunshot, Sam had leapt from the bed with dagger in hand and pushed the dresser with kerosene lamp over the entryway, blocking the door. The unlit kerosene lamp fell to the floor and broke. He moved away from the dresser now and positioned himself with his back to the opposite wall so that he could see in both directions if either boo hag dared to enter the room. Nothing came through the window, and Sam heard the second bullet fire in the darkness below.

In the hallway, he heard footsteps going down the stairs. They must have been the old man's because they were heavy thuds on the floor. He did not know where the old woman was. He waited in the dark, moonlit room. He held the dagger upraised, but he was now shaking violently.

Outside at the front entrance, Sani was crouched with a spear in either hand. He knew the old man would be the hardest to battle. The front door flew open, and the old man came out with the meat cleaver in hand and wearing nothing but undergarments. He rounded the corner and suddenly fell upon the waiting, upraised spear of the medicine man. The makeshift spear broke under the weight of the other man, and the startled old man swung the meat cleaver at the medicine man who let go of the spear and fell back to retreat. The stick was stuck in the man, and yet, he kept coming at Sani swinging the cleaver. Sani put his hands out. They glowed red to set a stream of fire toward the old man. The undergarments of the man caught fire, and he angrily swung more fiercely than ever.

Sani scrambled back, and picking up again the last remaining spear, he dodged the cleaver several times. When he found an opening, he tried again with the second spear, this time in the old man's leg bringing the man down. Then Sani used more fire, as much fire as he could muster. The old man had dropped the meat cleaver to the ground, and Sani hurried to pick it up and looked to the second story of the rock house. The old man was down and burning.

Kokopelli was standing outside in the moonlight with the rifle by his side and looking up into the second story window. He called out, "Sam!"

There was no answer. Sani gripped the cleaver tightly and

opened the front door to the rock house and went inside.

Sam heard Kokopelli call from down below, but Sam's eyes were glued to the dresser in front of the door that was slowly moving. He could hear the wood shift on the floor and saw a red-clawed hand reach through the slit in the door. It slowly curled around the door and pushed harder on the dresser.

"Let me in," he heard the witch say.

Sam said nothing. He held tightly to the dagger, but he was visibly shaking. He was in an extreme panic from having lain so long on the bed filled with dread.

He watched the dresser move more.

"Let me in," repeated the boo hag from the dark opening in the doorway. The boo hag was watching him through the door now. He was certain of that. "Let me in, or I'll eat your flesh." The boo hag cackled softly.

She pushed harder against the dresser, and now it slid across the floor and moved aside enough that she could enter the room. Sam held the dagger up and shifted, sliding across the room to the corner by the window.

The old woman was now skinless, red, and meaty and staring at him intently. She stepped into the room, but there were the broken glass shards on the floor from the kerosene lamp. She looked down and paused briefly, determining how to avoid getting cut.

The medicine man had run up the stairs and stopped at the top. The boo hag was in clear view at the end of the corridor and advancing into the bedroom. Sani had no time to think, so he pivoted from the stairs and turned into the corridor. Then he raised the meat cleaver with both hands up and over his head and threw it as hard as he could toward the boo hag. It made a soft whirring sound as it circled over and over again and struck dead center into the back of the boo hag. She fell forward into the room and onto the glass shards on the floor. But she continued to crawl toward Sam in the corner of the room. She slid arm over sickening meaty arm across the wood floor until she had reached his feet. She was on him now and then pulled herself up to attack him.

Sam raised his dagger and brought it down onto the hag. The hag fell onto him dead. Sam pushed himself violently out from under the boo hag and away toward the window. He looked out and saw Kokopelli standing there in the moonlight with the rifle by his side. Sani was now standing in the doorway looking at the boo hag on the floor. And Sam, who's nostrils filled with the smell of rotting flesh from the boo hag in the room, suddenly bent over and slid down against the wall and to the wood floor, panting.

Chapter Fourteen: On the Outskirts of Silver Springs

Sani helped Sam back down out of the upstairs rooms of the rock house, and together they headed out the front door. Sam sat down on the rock wall, and Kokopelli came around the front of the rock house with his empty rifle by his side.

"We must make sure the bodies are dead. I'm going to finish burning the two outside. We need to scavenge for safe food and weapons. Sam, we'll take that wagon, and you will show me how to hitch the horses to it. We also need clothing because we are heading into the mountains. Sam, I know you've been through a lot, but I need the two of you to go inside and gather what you can. Afterward, we'll burn everything so no traveler will ever return here again."

Sam and Kokopelli understood. They went inside while the medicine man worked quickly outside. Kokopelli found a blanket in the living room and unfolded it and put it on the kitchen table. They scavenged the cabinets and cupboards for any untainted foods they could take along. They placed what they could on the blanket. Sam opened a large closet off to the side of the kitchen and stepped back. Inside, on the top shelf of the closet was a collection of skulls. He shuddered and looked below and found coats and various garments they could take. To the right, he also noticed an upturned wooden handle. He lifted it out of the closet to reveal an ax. It appeared to be silver-plated and sharp. He took it as well.

When they had placed their items on the table, they looked at each other and nodded and then reluctantly headed upstairs. The door to the travelers' bedroom was still open, but they turned and opened the first door at the top of the stairs. It led into the other boo hag's room. They scanned the room quickly, and then Kokopelli went to the closet. He opened the door and saw some clothes that he took, both for men and women. As he was reaching into the closet, he looked to the right in the secret hidden portion of the closet. His blood ran cold then. He slowly pushed the clothes back to reveal several skins hanging—a variety of skins. He went back to the clothes and quickly yanked what he needed off the hangers and shut the closet.

Sam was heading down the corridor to the third room when Kokopelli said, "Sam, we got what we need. Let's go." He didn't tell Sam what he found in the closet. He just wanted out of there as fast as possible.

They gathered up everything in their blanket, tied it, and headed out of the house. Sani had already made quick work of disposing of the bodies and was in the red barn freeing the horses. He freed all but Sam's horse and one other for the wagon. Kokopelli then put water into the large metal bucket from the pump and watered the two horses while the medicine man and Sam pushed out the wagon. Kokopelli watched as they worked fast to hitch the two remaining horses. All three then loaded the wagon with the supplies. Sam got on the wagon, though he was not familiar with driving one. He and Kokopelli turned the wagon and headed down the path to the main road.

Sani went to the red barn first and set it on fire. Then he went to the rock house and went upstairs to the room where the boo hag lay on the floor. He knelt and looked at the spilled kerosene. He quickly sparked it and stepped back. The kerosene fire spread fast, and Sani walked out of the burning building and down the path to the waiting wagon at the main road. He climbed onto the back of the wagon.

Later, Sani sat in the dark on the wagon holding the reins. He looked down the empty main road and waited for the others to fetch Mai and Kai with the horses and Izou. When they were all loaded up and all the horses were securely tied to the back of the wagon, they circled the wagon and headed north to Silver Springs. No one talked much. And when they passed the burning buildings up the path, they whipped the reins to make the horses go faster. The wagon thumped and creaked on the open road, but it was pleasant to be riding together and no longer walking. Not much was said at all. Everyone's hearts were heavy, including Mai's, though she knew not what the others had been through. She'd seen the burning buildings, and that was enough to know it was not good.

They neared the old west town of Silver Springs in the early morning, and all were relieved to see the lights of civilization in the distance, though it was foreign. They encamped on a hilltop away from the main road but within view of the lights, which seemed to comfort them. They built a fire and ate some food that had been scavenged. They took care of Kai and Izou, and then they bedded down to rest. Mai kept watch this time and lay her back against a tree and watched the people beginning to move at dawn down in the town of Silver Springs. The events of the night before seemed to deeply change the attitudes of her other companions. They seemed weary and world-worn. She petted Izou on her lap and thought that she might ask Kokopelli to play his flute to help everyone feel better as they continued on their journey. She did love his music.

They rested in that spot for an entire day, worn out as they were and in need of replenished good spirits. Kokopelli did eventually play his flute for the others, and it did liven the mood again and make the others smile. Mai and Sam bonded over playing with Kai. The two had grown quite close over the trip, and Mai secretly found Sam to be handsome and strong. She smiled at him often. Sam, in turn, liked her protective nature with Kai.

In the afternoon, they changed into the new garments from the rock house. Sam and Kokopelli went into Silver Springs to sell the silver-plated ax but could not find a reasonable buyer and so returned empty-handed. They rested there overnight and then in the morning were gone.

They were headed to the final burned smudge on the map ...

the third trial. The idea of another ordeal hung heavy on their hearts. The smudge on the map indicated a spot between the towns of Silver Springs and Creede, and it looked like a difficult journey via a narrow road through mountainous terrain and rocky cliffs and deep forests of pines and aspens. The trail wound like a snake through the mountain pass, and the smudge was not far from the road, just a little north into the mountains. They were glad to have warmer clothes now because they would need them. The symbol on the map near the burned smudge was odd. It appeared to be a cave. They sat in the wagon as it slowly wound up the mountainous pass. The wagon lurched and thumped and rocked as it went.

Chapter Fifteen: Closer

Neqael looked at the remains of the burned buildings. He sniffed the grounds for the tracks of the travel party and smelled something near the bushes that must have been human or humanlike. Whatever happened here, it was fierce. *Good*, he thought. He was up for a challenge, and these humans had proven quite resourceful. But the saber-toothed tiger was on a whole other level of cunning. He knew this, and he growled to himself with immense pleasure at his work thus far. Hashkeh Naabah would be proud.

The Smilodon shape-shifter knew he was close to them now. He picked up their scent on the winds and ground leading down the main road. They left too many obvious indicators. They had taken one of these human contraptions, a wheeled vehicle, and Neqael headed down the main road, following the tracks of the wheels. There were very few travelers out and about, so it was easy to remain stealthy and quiet. He found their spot at the base of the tree on the hilltop overlooking Silver Springs, and he prowled the area briefly. Then he turned north and then east again, following their trail up into the mountain pass. He grinned wickedly to himself. *I've got them.* The hunter thought to himself that it would not be long now.

Chapter Sixteen: A Tragic Backstory

Many, many years ago, around the year 1637, there lived a young and brave Ute warrior named Cinthalu. He was a mighty and adept horseman and quite skilled with bow and spear. Although he was from the Weeminuche band, he had fallen in love with a Mouache woman and settled with her family. They had two daughters and a son. The Mouache woman was also the daughter of the chief, a man well respected by the community and various other trading tribes.

The tribe lived in the southern region of Colorado but resided at the time in the Santa Fe de Nuevo Mexico Federation of the Spanish. One day a warring faction of the Apache along with Spanish soldiers raided the tribe while Cinthalu was out hunting for deer with two other fellow warriors. Under the orders of the Santa Fe governor, Luis de Rosas, eighty Mouache women and children were stolen that day to be forced into slave labor at textile shops in the south. Cinthalu returned to the encampment to find it burned and destroyed and many slaughtered. He found the body of the Mouache chief, who had vowed to convert to Christianity if his people would be spared. The chief's throat had been slit, and his cold hand was still clutching a rosary from Friar Benivedes of the Santa Fe Chapel of La Conquistadora Virgin Mary. His vows had been to no avail, as the greed of the Spaniards had overcome their compassion.

Cinthalu took the chief to the ancestral burial grounds and faced his head east as was proper. On that day, with the death of his wife's father and the enslavement of his wife and children, Cinthalu vowed revenge. He stayed near the burial grounds and called to the powers of the dark. He stayed there until nightfall. He heard a voice in the forest that night that resembled the voice of the chief. It mimicked the voice but was not his. Whatever the creature was, it moved fast and deliberately around the warrior who now faced the woods in the dark alone with buffalo hide shield and spear. The attack was so fast, he had no time to counter and was sharply clawed. As he lay upon the forest floor, it moved over him. The creature was nine feet tall and ghastly thin with long limbs, single-toed feet, and sharp talon claws for hands. It had no hair and bright yellow eyes. Its teeth were sharp, nasty fangs, and as it paused over him to sniff his scent, a long blue tongue flicked from its mouth. It bit him and then left.

Cinthalu had a fever and chills for three days afterwards. The thirst and hunger inside him had become insatiable. His sense of vision became infrared at night, and he could smell, see, and hear things from far off. And he changed ... He mutated. He became craven, in need of a feeding frenzy. And as he wandered the forests, he began to capture and feast on other creatures. But he craved more. He desired human meat like a cannibal and had become the dreaded windigo.

This was not the revenge he had intended with tragic despair, but he wandered north into the southwest Colorado mountains until he found an abandoned cave in a rocky mountain cliffside surrounded by deep, dense forest. And that cave was just northwest of the place that would become Creede. Over the years, he would hibernate for months or even decades at a time and then feast. This became his life.

He emerged from the cave entrance from a thirty-year hibernation. His body was gaunt, and he could feel his ribs and bones through his pale white skin. He stalked and attacked a settler mining party off the pass, ripping through their tents as they slept at night. He feasted for a while on their remains until he smelled something on the winds. Something was approaching from the pass. He paused eating. He hid the remains in the woods, storing them for food for the approaching winter, which would be cold and harsh, and he prepared for his next hunt.

Chapter Seventeen: Beware of the Forest

"Ishmael meets this man named Queequeg, and together they join the *Pequod* ship owned by Captain Ahab. Ahab is in search of a mysterious white whale called Moby-Dick," explained Sam to the others. The journey via wagon was long and bumpy, and he wanted to keep their minds occupied on something else. They had tried listening to Kokopelli's flute for a while, and everyone seemed happy with that. Even Sani, sitting beside Sam on the bench while he drove the wagon, smiled at the music. But there had been a lull in the conversation after days of travel through the steep mountainous pass. Sam had asked the others about their village, and they spoke of many things related to the place. Sam, in turn, told them about Stoney Creek and about his life with the barge master. After admiring the scenery and pointing out various foraging plant species, they engaged for a while in a pleasant exchange and talking about the weather. They had started to sit in silence as the wagon lurched and creaked and bumped along.

Mai sat in the wagon amid the gear and supplies across from Kokopelli, and she slowly mouthed the word in English, "Queequeg ... Queeeeee ... queg," and she laughed. "Yes, I like this word." And she said it again. "Queequeg. And this is someone's name?"

"Yes, a sailor on the ocean—Polynesian, actually."

"Pol ... y ... nesian. What is this? Polynesian?"

"It is a place far away across the ocean."

"Ocean?"

Sam grimaced. This was more awkward than he thought it would be. "Yes, ocean. The many waters."

"Oh, yes," said Sani. "We know this thing you call ocean, but what is a whale, and why is it white?"

"A whale is an ocean mammal like a fish," explained Sam, and he motioned with his free hand something very big. But the others did not quite get how large.

"Ah," said the medicine man proudly, understanding and explaining to Kokopelli and Mai. "Large like a bass."

"Uh ..." began Sam, but the medicine man was smiling now, and so he flicked the reins and looked ahead down the pass. "Not quite." Sam muttered under his breath. "Bigger," he said.

"Bigger?" The medicine man's eyes got larger and then suspicious. "How big?"

Sam looked around the scenery to find something equivalent to the size of the whale. He couldn't find anything as large, so he pointed to something close enough. "See that tree there?"

Sani nodded, following him.

"That big."

"Nah," said the medicine man, shaking his head and eyeing Sam incredulously. Then, with great suspicion, he added, "No, no ... I don't believe this. This is folklore—a myth."

"No, seriously! There are fish in the ocean as big as that. They even are said to swallow men." Sam then began to explain the story of Jonah and the whale from the Bible.

"O ... cean," said Mai in the back again. "O ... cean."

Sani listened intently to Sam's story of Jonah, but he laughed at several moments. "You're saying this immortal sent this big fish"—he held out his hands wide and mockingly—"to eat a man just to spit him out. Ha-ha. Why would he do such a thing? Silly stories you have."

Sam smiled halfway and shrugged. "Yeah, I suppose when you look at it this way."

Sani tried to reassure Sam of their friendship "We have these types of stories too at the cliff village." He pointed proudly at himself. "I too am quite the storyteller."

"Yes, he is," confirmed Kokopelli and Mai. Together, they recounted the story of his father, Fire Spirit. They also spoke about Spider Mother.

The wagon continued to plod and bump along the road. They were fortunate that the wagon wheels stayed strong and did not break on the journey. As the others talked, Mai took off her left sandal and inspected her foot. She had a nasty bubbled blister on her heel, and it appeared that it could fester. She would need to keep an eye on it.

Kokopelli looked at her feet and said, "Mai, you alright? That looks like it hurts. Do you have any more?"

Mai slipped off her right sandal to reveal a few more blisters.

"I've got a few too," said Kokopelli as he motioned to his feet.

The medicine man caught what they had said, and he turned on the bench to look as well. He was concerned. "We'll need to be on the lookout for the herbal medicines." He nodded to Kokopelli and Mai, and they discussed what this bush looked like: twiggy with spiky yellow flowers. He explained for the others and the benefit of Sam. "We take the leaves and crush them." He motioned using a rock and bowl to grind and smash something to fine paste.

"Oh, we have something we use for blisters. We call that witch hazel. It is a liquid, like water," said Sam.

"Hm," said the medicine man, looking at Sam and nodding. Then he looked to the road again and nodded to himself as if thinking over this new information. "Witch hazel ... you name it after a witch....like the ones we encountered earlier?" he questioned, raising his left eyebrow.

"Yeah," said Sam.

The medicine man was thinking more and more that these people on the other side of the Snake River were quite odd. But he kept that opinion to himself.

There was a big rock in the road that could bust one of the wagon wheels, so Sam carefully maneuvered the wagon around it. They continued on their way and spoke more about various other matters. Kokopelli and Mai each told jokes, and then the flute was played some more to pass the time. Izou was out of his satchel and running the length of the wagon bed, scurrying here and there. Occasionally, he would come to rest beside Kokopelli, and Kokopelli would reach down and gently pet him. Kokopelli gave Izou some water and a little food from the supplies.

Baby Kai was often awake and looking around while lying in the bed of the wagon on blankets. Sometimes he slept, but mostly, he was a good baby. They often stopped to care for him, feeding and changing and holding him some before continuing on the trek down the road. They had made a makeshift awning over the area of the wagon bed where the baby lay in order to protect his skin and face from too much sun.

It was becoming colder in the higher elevations of the mountain area. They made sure that baby Kai was warm and comfortable with the blankets. They were grateful for the garments they had, though the clothes felt awkward and uncomfortable at times. Mai repeatedly tripped over the hem of her long dress.

They stopped at night several times just off the road, unhitched the horses, and left the wagon close to the side. Thus far on the road, they had only encountered one stagecoach and a few lone riders on horses ... nothing much to be greatly concerned about. At one point early on after leaving the Silver Springs region, they did pass a chuckwagon caravan, but that was all. They spent a lot of time admiring the mountains and cliffs and the tall ponderosa pines and white aspens. And there were times when they each felt to themselves that they were being watched. But they just shrugged this off and kept along together headed down the road toward the final destination—the third trial, a cave off the pass. They would need to abandon the wagon soon, probably quite soon, and head straight north.

Kokopelli, Sam, and Sani had not talked much of the second test. Hopefully, this one would be all right.

They came across a steep wood and steel bridge spanning a ravine. They decided to stop here, as the medicine man pointed out some herbal plants in the ravine below to their right. Perhaps they had some brief time to do a little foraging.

At the west entrance to the bridge, they pulled over to the south side. They laid a blanket on the grass in the shade of some trees and sat down on it. They stopped to eat there, take care of Kai, and relax some. The third marker on the map was not far away now. Mai took Kai and asked Kokopelli to help secure him around her abdomen again. They secured the snug blanket at her back and waist. She told the others she intended to go down the ravine a short distance and examine the herbs they had seen from the bridge. Meanwhile, Sam and Kokopelli began loading things back up in the wagon on the bridge. Sani offered to go with Mai and for their protection, and in case they ran across any wildlife, he grabbed the ax from the wagon. Besides the dagger, it was their only means of protection.

They carefully stepped down the rocky, pebbled hillside beneath the bridge. The medicine man held Mai's arm at several points to keep her from slipping. They headed to the herbal patch, and Mai found the twiggy plant with spiked flowers and began picking leaves and flowers to place in her satchel. She slowly moved along the ravine heading back toward the bridge, and the medicine man was also inspecting various plants to be used on their journey. He was looking south, and there was some distance between the two. Mai kept moving and humming to herself. She checked on Kai who was looking comfortable and happy snuggled beside her. She thought she noted another patch of spiked yellow flowers in the shadow of the bridge, and so she crossed just under the bridge and out of sight from above where Sam and Kokopelli kept loading and going through supplies.

"Mai! I found some more! Come quick!" she heard Sam say. The voice was coming from the north just past the bridge. The voice was low, and when she seemed to hesitate, it started again. "Hurry! I want to show you what I found!"

Mai briefly touched Kai who was happily looking at her with big brown eyes. She headed under the bridge into the darkened shadow and started up the ravine on the north side toward the direction of Sam's voice.

Sani had been studying an assortment of cone flowers and black-eyed Susans when he looked back in the direction of where he thought Mai was standing. She was not there, and he quickly scanned around and saw her and Kai moving up the ravine past the bridge. He swung around and headed her way with the ax in hand and pointed downward. Kokopelli and Sam were still working on the wagon, and the medicine man was wondering why Mai had wandered so far onto the other side.

"Mai," he called. He motioned with his free hand for her to come back.

She looked at him momentarily but then looked at the trees. Ignoring him, she kept struggling to get up the ravine with Kai and her satchel. She reached the top and went past a large coniferous evergreen. The medicine man kept moving her way and made it to the bridge. Mai had moved behind the evergreen, and suddenly, he saw a strange movement. From behind the tree, he saw her fall back and land hard on the grass, hitting her head on the ground. All he could see was her face turned toward him and a sprawled arm. She appeared knocked out by a rock or something, as there was a wound with blood over her temple. One moment he could see her head and arm, and the next she was violently and quickly dragged out of sight behind the tree by something.

Sani began to run toward the evergreen tree with his ax. He quickly struggled up the rocks of the ravine, pushing to the top and toward the spot where he had seen Mai fall. He heard the baby's cry, but it was not close by, and as he rounded the tree, there was no one there. He looked north through the trees to the distress cries of Kai and saw the creature. It was moving exceedingly fast through the woods. Mai's limp body with Kai was being held like a prize in the arms of a strange gaunt and white, skeletal beast that appeared to stand nine feet tall. It was running quickly, and Mai's head hung down from its arms, for she had been knocked unconscious.

There was no time to holler at Sam or Kokopelli for help, so the medicine man took off in pursuit through the trees alone. But the creature was so fast, and try as he might, he could not catch it or keep up with it. But Kai, thankfully, kept crying, so when he lost sight of the creature, he followed the sound of the baby. He kept running through the strange and foreign woods, up hills and down, across dry creek beds, and through the thick hedges of trees. He was growing winded, and the ax was heavy on his right arm, but he needed it. He kept running until suddenly, he no longer heard the baby. *Kai! Kai!* he thought. He turned in a full circle in the unfamiliar forest, wide-eyed and looking all around for the creature and listening closely for the baby.

Off to his left, through the woods, he saw something moving stealthy and extremely fast and heading north as well. A giant, ferocious beast with sharpened saber teeth. It was much larger than a mountain lion. It had dark brown fur, and it wasn't just moving at full gait; it was silently and extremely quickly charging with lightning speed toward something up ahead. *Mai and Kai,* thought the medicine man. Now he followed the only thing he knew to follow: the strange predator beast in the woods. He took off after it, tearing through the branches and woods.

Ahead, he could hear something ... an attack, a vicious battle between two violent creatures. He kept running with the ax, though his heart pounded and thudded hard in his chest. He now heard a terrible shriek followed by a massive roaring and then the breaking of trees and something hitting the ground very hard. This was followed by more sounds—growls, shrieks, roars, breaking trees, and crashes—and then he saw a large boulder fly into the woods up ahead, knocking out a swath of two or three trees.

Then, the creatures came into view. They were fighting, not just fighting but battling to the death, viciously tearing and clawing at each other, pouncing on one another, and biting into each other's flesh with their fangs. Sani could see now, with great fear, that the white monster was a windigo. It was hideously misshapen, large, and fast with sharp talon claws that it swung violently at the other predator's throat. The other predator beast, though, was also fast and dodged the attacks, moving swiftly left and right of the windigo and forcing it farther north. The medicine man looked north as well and saw the body of Mai and Kai lying across the rooted base of a tree. Kai was crying. The tree was ten feet from a sudden drop-off of a rocky, mountainous cliff. Across from the cliff was a rock plateau, and on its west flank at the base was a blackened crevice ... a cave. The medicine man knew in that moment that this creature, this windigo, was the final test. He recognized the shape of the cave, and he knew the creature was taking Mai and Kai to the cave and he must stop them. The medicine man gripped his ax and began to skirt the battle scene to reach Mai and Kai.

The two creatures were still viciously attacking one another, but the big cat had managed to push the windigo back toward the ledge. The windigo picked up the cat after it lunged toward him and hurled it into a nearby tree. The cat was hurt but got up and advanced toward the windigo, growling menacingly low and baring its teeth. The windigo stepped back three feet from the ledge, looking scared. The saber-toothed cat, thinking it had the upper hand, roared and then leapt straight at the windigo, attempting to push it off the drop-off of the rock cliff.

The windigo then smiled cunningly, baring his yellowed

fangs, and vaulted the big cat over him. And just like that, the saber-toothed tiger plummeted below, over the edge of the cliff, falling farther and farther down onto the jutting rocks beneath.

The windigo turned toward Mai and Kai. Sani rushed out of the woods with ax in hand and prepared to block the windigo's path to the others. Baby Kai was still crying, but Mai was unconscious. The windigo advanced. The medicine man swung the ax, and the windigo quickly dodged it. He swung again. The windigo sidestepped it. The windigo appeared to be amused until he came a little too close and was met with a cut on his arm. The windigo howled in pain at the cut and retreated. The cut was not large, but it was mysteriously smoking.

Sani looked at the silver plate on the ax. Sani then advanced on the windigo toward the cliff, swinging the ax as he went. But the windigo knocked the ax out of his hand with his sharp talon claws. The ax fell off to the right and into the woods. Sani and the windigo faced off against each other near the cliff. The windigo tried to frighten the medicine man by shrieking and howling. Sani did the only thing he could do. He moved his right and left hands toward the windigo; red sparks burst from his hands, and he blasted the windigo with all the firepower he had. The windigo nearly went over the cliff. He was visibly shocked and frightened at first. Then he shrieked a massive, violent noise that resounded through the nearby forest and looked with terrible anger at the medicine man. He bared his yellow fanged mouth and barreled toward Sani, hitting his full weight into the man and tackling him to the ground. Then he flung the medicine man wide and hard into the woods. Sani reached out to stop himself, but his head hit hard against a tree base, and he landed with a cold, knocked-out thud onto the forest floor.

The windigo shrieked again and snarled in victory with his hideous visage and jutted fangs. He stepped away from the cliff and began walking slowly and deliberately into the woods and toward the body of the man whom he intended to feast on first. But the baby was the real prize to the windigo. He had not had baby in such a long time.

As the windigo passed a few trees; in the distance, off to the right and out of the corner of his eye, he sensed something in the woods—something dark and ominous. The windigo noted that the wind had grown still. The birds of the forest were not making noise. In fact, there was suddenly no noise at all, only sudden silence. The windigo turned to look at the dark entity in the woods and blinked once. He opened his eyes again, and the dark watcher was beside him. And the ghost took the windigo.

Sam and Kokopelli were moving in the woods north from the main road searching for the medicine man, Mai, and Kai. The others had all disappeared, and the young men were worried. They were calling to Mai and Sani when they heard a terrifying shriek, a bloodcurdling shriek of a hurt beast or creature in the woods. And then, they heard nothing at all.

Chapter Eighteen: Unexpected Visitors

Sam and Kokopelli were searching the forest. They called out to the others as they tracked and continued north. They heard nothing. Overhead, through the boughs of the trees, they could see that the clouds were growing overcast. As they felt the first raindrops fall, they looked at each other and called out again for Mai and Sani, this time more urgently. They had left the wagon and horses at the main road. It did not matter now. All that mattered was finding the others.

Sani lay crumpled under the tree where he had fallen. A raindrop fell upon his cheek ... then a few more, and he stirred slowly. He raised his hand to feel his face, and his fingers touched the wetness. More and more raindrops began to fall. He was in pain. His back and head were hurting, but he managed to get into a position where he lifted himself slightly and looked around. Mai and Kai were off to the side of the clearing, and just beyond them in the distance rose the jagged, mountainous rocks with the cave entrance to the left. The rain began to descend on the clearing. Mai and Kai were both quiet.

Sani raised himself to his feet, and he was in a great deal of pain. He touched his back and ribs, clutching his side as he moved toward Mai. When he got to her, he knelt down and checked Kai. Kai was startled but alive and crying. He was bundled against Mai who had a massive concussion bump on her forehead. The blood had pooled around it and was matting. Sani bent down and touched her shoulder and then tried to wake her. She did not move. He checked to make sure she was breathing. He felt her heartbeat; it was slow and strong. She was alive.

The rains were coming down around them and getting everything wet. He shook her again and again until her eyes fluttered and she opened them. She seemed to be trying to focus them, and then she turned her face to look at him. Her left hand came up to touch the blankets over Kai. She looked down at Kai and looked again at the medicine man and said, "Kai is alright? My head hurts."

The rain was getting on her face too, and the medicine man gingerly touched around her head wound. He took off his shirt, tore the arm sleeve, and then attempted to bandage the wound with the cloth and clear the blood with the remaining shirt. He tied the bandage as best he could and then helped them to sit up slowly. Kai was crying now. They were alone in the clearing overlooking the cliff. The rain was falling. The sky had darkened.

The medicine man motioned to the cave and said, "We'll have to make it over there. It's too far to go back in this weather. Lightning and thunder may come."

They got up together and began making their way to the cave. Amid the rain and the thunder, they heard the calls from the forest. They called back to Sam and Kokopelli, and it was not long before the travel party was reunited in the rain. The group then headed to the cave. Sam helped the medicine man to walk, and Kokopelli helped Mai with Kai. Little Izou darted out of Kokopelli's pouch to climb up on his shoulder despite the wind and the rain, but when Izou saw the overcast clouds, he hurried back to the satchel.

They were soaked, but they made it to the cave entrance and went inside. They huddled together, shivering at the front of the cave. No one wanted to venture farther in, but they needed wood for a fire. The medicine man explained to Kokopelli and Sam that this was the cave of a windigo but he was gone. Where he had gone, no one knew. Sam and Kokopelli went deeper into the cave to find timber. They found some sticks here and there, but when they began to find what looked like human bones, they came back to the entrance. They had enough to start a little fire. Outside, the rain was pouring on the rocks.

They lit the little fire and waited for the rain to cease. They then talked about what had happened. Pools of water gathered outside the cave. They huddled together, and eventually, the rain stopped. The fire did not last long, and they were far from their supplies, gear, and wagon. All the travel party members were downtrodden and despairing, but they waited together. Kokopelli untied Kai and held him. Fortunately, Mai had the satchel with the drinking pouch, and they were able to calm and soothe Kai to sleep.

As they huddled in the dark at the front entrance of the windigo cave with the fire going out and not knowing what else to do next, a single, solitary spider descended from a single web string down onto the floor across from them. And it spoke.

"Tsintah sent me. You have passed the three tests. He promised you that he would provide you a gift at the end of the final test ... and here I am, Spider Mother returned." The spider said politely.

An astonished Mai, Kokopelli, and Sam just looked at the spider. But the medicine man said with exhaustion, "Thank you."

Again, the spider seemed to be pleased with the answer.

"It was not easy finding you, but I have ... with Tsintah's help, of course. We are close to the town of Creede, a mining community. It is there that we will find your father, Sani ... in the mines. There is a silver mine within a day's journey from here. We will take the elevator down one thousand feet into the mountain, and from there, it is a short distance to the cavern where your father waits. The miners dug deep in the mountain but not deep enough. They dug a hole farther into the cavern, but the men who went into the hole did not reappear, and for whatever reason now, the mine is now abandoned. Your father waits there imprisoned in the darkness. We will free him, but we must be careful. He is guarded by a giant bat in the cavern."

"A bat?" asked Sani.

“Yes, a very large, carnivorous bat that sees in the dark,” said Spider Mother.

“And you know how to defeat this bat?” asked Kokopelli.

The spider shifted. “No, not me, per say … but he does.” The spider lifted a leg to point out of the cave. The others followed her movement to see Tsintah standing still in his cloak in the shadows, unbothered by the rains dripping down from the heavens.

Chapter Nineteen: One Thousand-Plus Feet Underground

After a day's journey into the mountains, the travel party surveyed the abandoned mining site. The site was built into a mountainside many miles from the town of Creede. There were three wooden cabins located on the premises and one lean-to shelter with a metal contraption and pulley system. Tsintah explained that this was the elevator that would take them down deep into the mountain. He motioned to the lever that would start the pulley system. Tsintah explained that the elevator would drop to the bottom, and then they would need to follow a network of tunnels in search of the location of the hidden cavern.

Tsintah explained, "The elevator will not be able to hold all of us, and we need someone to stay above to be our lookout. I recommend that Kokopelli, Sani, and myself, along with Spider Mother take the elevator down. This steel conveyance will hold us, but it must go down one thousand feet below. I warn you now that the descent in the elevator is not for the weak of heart."

The others nodded. Sam and Mai agreed to stay above with Kai as lookouts and to start and stop the elevator.

"We must check the cabins first to see if they are occupied. If not, Sam and Mai should stay in that one." He pointed to the largest one with windows on all sides to provide an excellent vantage point.

"We'll gather what mining gear we can find as well. Probably most of it is gone."

They slowly entered the mining site area and spread out, searching each of the three cabins. The place was abandoned and mostly cleared out, though they did find one busted but usable lantern in the large cabin. They also found a very large roll of sturdy rope in the lean-to. Tsintah slung this rope upon his shoulder. He had also placed Spider Mother secure in his side satchel.

They walked over to the elevator and found the gates locked. All but Mai and Kai with Izou scaled the fences one by one. Tsintah motioned for Kokopelli and Sani and himself to enter the mining elevator, which had room for only a few men. It was an uncomfortable feeling for the men, as the elevator swayed lightly in the breeze above the tremendous drop. They each held their breath as Sam pulled the lever and released the brake that would begin their slow descent via pulley system down into the mountain.

Tsintah, Kokopelli, and Sani looked up startled as they cleared the surface and went deeper and deeper down. They could see the rock walls of the elevator shaft on all four sides. The drop was dark, yet they stayed standing with arms and gear inside the little elevator cart that creaked and moaned. Farther and farther down they went, and they all stayed resolutely still, yet internally, Kokopelli and Sani were quite afraid. One thousand feet in a rickety old elevator was a very long time indeed, as each second ticked away and the cart inched farther down inch by inch by painstaking inch in the dark. The temperature was dropping too, and it felt different inside the mountain—no winds, no breeze, just stillness and a dampness in the air.

At last, the elevator landed with a jolt on something at the bottom—the dirt floor of the mine. Tsintah took the busted lantern in his hand, and in the dark, he managed to carefully hand it over to Kokopelli.

“Start the lantern candle with fire,” said Tsintah to Sani.

Very gently, Sani sparked some flames from his left hand. The three looked at each other in the dark and then looked at the busted lantern that Kokopelli opened. Gently, the medicine man touched flame to the candle inside. Kokopelli carefully secured the top of the lantern.

“This candle won’t last long,” said Tsintah. “We will need to move quickly.”

Tsintah opened the elevator door and stepped slightly down onto the dirt floor, and the others followed, making the elevator sway side to side just a little.

They were in a tunnel area. To their right was a rail cart and solid wall. To their left was a darkened tunnel. They went left. The tunnel was not wide, so they had to move one by one following the rails. They journeyed left for a while before they entered a large chamber of rock. When Tsintah held the lantern up, they could see various beams where miners had worked up the chamber following the silver vein. They continued on to a fork in the tunnels and determined whether to go left or right. They reasoned that the Fire Spirit would be deep in the mountain, so they chose to go left again. They continued on. The candle began to lower more as they entered a room that must have housed donkeys to carry the carts of silver and gems, for there were stalls to their right that were now empty.

They walked on in the eerie darkness and quiet, and Kokopelli, who was wide-eyed and fearful at this point, was beginning to feel a little claustrophobic. They passed blast walls and old pickaxes for the rocks. Chamber after chamber, tunnel after tunnel, they went until each worried they may have made the wrong turn. The candle had burned down to the final quarter at this point, wax dripping onto the lantern base.

It was Kokopelli who spotted the dark hole to the right of the last tunnel. They had come to a dead end and were worried they would need to circle back when Kokopelli stepped back and nearly fell into something. Tsintah turned the lantern toward the place where Kokopelli tripped, and there by the edge near the rock wall was a four-foot-wide hole, just big enough for one man to enter.

Tsintah took the lamp and held it over the hole. Sani took a tiny rock and dropped it down the hole. They did not hear a sound for two seconds and then heard a thud as it hit something on the ground.

They had the rope with them to enter the hole, but they reasoned that they had passed some ladders a while back in the tunnels. They went back the way they had come to the large chamber, pulled a ladder down, and carried it back. They speculated that perhaps the ladder would be long enough, and they carefully lowered it down into the hole. It fit, but barely. Kokopelli carefully positioned it against the wall inside the little hole. The candle in the lantern was just about out. One by one, the men slowly dangled from the edge of the deep hole until they reached foothold on the topmost rung of the ladder. Then each one slowly went down, rung by rung, into the pitch-black darkness. Tsintah was holding the busted lantern, but as all three dropped into the hole and came to the bottom, the candle in the lantern flickered and died.

This was new dark territory. They did not know for sure what lay ahead, only that miners who had gone into the hole before never came out. They first listened in the darkness all around them. Tsintah knelt and put the lantern on the ground. He straightened and motioned to the medicine man to light his hand aflame, and Sani did.

They all looked around them. There was a passageway leading from the ladder deep into a very narrow tunnel. The medicine man led the way this time as they went spelunking through the deep crevices of the dark mountain.

Kokopelli's claustrophic heart was beginning to pound, and he wanted to be out of the mountain. He worried for a moment about earth movements. What if the tunnels collapsed and they were stuck in there? But they kept going one by one until they neared an opening at the end, which led into a massive cavern. The drop-off from the tunnel to the floor of the giant cavern appeared to be ten feet.

Tsintah motioned to the medicine man to be quiet and put

out his flamed hands. He told Kokopelli and the medicine man, "We will have to do this part without the aid of light. Sani, extinguish the flame. One by one, we must clear the tunnel and jump. When you land, roll to your right and get near the wall as close as possible. We don't know what is inside the cavern. Ready? Let's go."

Sani stopped the flame in his hand, and the darkness became pitch-black all around them. He moved forward to the edge of the tunnel until he was ready to jump out, feeling his way with his hands. The others followed close behind him. He said, "I'm going to jump." And he leapt out of the tunnel. For a second, he was in the air, and then he landed hard and rolled to the right. He found the wall and placed himself as close as possible to it. His heart was beating loudly in his chest, but other than that, the only sounds he heard were the movements of Kokopelli and Tsintah. They too rolled and came to the wall beside him, groping for the rock. Sani helped them to get beside him in the dark.

They sat there for a while and listened. They realized they were not alone in the great cavern as they began to hear occasional fluttering noises and squeaks.

"Bats," whispered Tsintah. "Many, many bats."

Chapter Twenty: Bat Attack

They sat motionless against the wall listening to the cavern in the dark. All they could hear was the fluttering and squeaks.

"What do we do now?" whispered Kokopelli.

"Here comes the tricky part," replied Tsintah. "The bats already know we are here." They remembered that Tsintah could speak to animals. "They are studying us now, in the dark, determining how much of a threat we are." He paused. "I have limited abilities to speak to animals. I can hear them but not as one large group. There are many of them here, though, and they are communicating about us. We can't move past them until we encounter Niyol."

"Niyol?" the medicine man asked.

"Yes, the alpha—the giant bat in the cave. He knows we are here too." Tsintah paused again and sighed. "All right, let's get this over with. Time to face the bats. Stay close to me. Hold onto my arm, Kokopelli, and, in turn, Sani, hold on to Kokopelli. One, two, and three." And with that, he stepped out from the wall, and the others followed.

The bats fluttered overhead much louder now, and it seemed to the three men that there were at least a thousand or more waiting in that cavern overhead, watching and waiting. The more they advanced in the pitch-black, the more the bats squeaked and fluttered until they had taken five steps into the cavern.

Tsintah stopped. "They're coming!" he said. "Use your flame, Sani!"

The medicine man let go of Kokopelli, put both hands high above his head, and set them aflame just in time. A great mass of black bats flew straight at them, but when the bats saw the flames, the bats veered cautiously to the left in one fell swoop. There were not just a thousand but maybe two or three thousand. They swarmed high overhead and threatened to attack again. They came right at the travelers and then veered hard to the right fluttering, and squeaking past the three men. They flew higher once more and then came down again, this time encircling the three men who now had their backs to each other. The bats flew around and around, fluttering and squeaking. It was a frightening sight to behold.

Tsintah looked over his should at Kokopelli and said calmly and quickly, "Kokopelli! Play your flute. Hit the highest pitched note you can! Do it fast!"

Kokopelli fumbled for his flute, put it to his mouth, and looked at the bats that were encircling and threatening to attack. He closed his eyes and played the highest note on his flute. He squeezed his lips tightly and played as loudly as he could.

Upon hearing the sound, the mass of bats broke up, fluttering and squeaking and making a terrible racket, and flew high into the overhead spaces of the cavern. Warily, they watched the new strangers in the room. Kokopelli continued to play the high note, and the last few straggler bats flew up to the lofts of the cavern.

Sani lighted the flames in his hands again. They looked overhead to the masses upon masses of fluttering bats until their eyes alighted on a very large, looming dark shadow in the depths of the cavern to the left. It opened its yellow eyes to look directly at them. The creature was hanging upside down like the other bats but was the most enormous, monstrous bat Kokopelli or Sani had ever encountered. It spread wide its long, leathery bat wings with sharp claws. It fluttered them once, twice ... and then looked directly at Tsintah.

It spoke. "To what do I owe this great honor, Tsintah? Why make your presence known here?"

And Tsintah answered, "You already know why I've come, Niyol. Fire Spirit."

The bat laughed a deep-hearted and sinister laugh. It fluttered its wings and then left its perch in the dark and slammed its hard, gigantic body onto the ground five feet in front of the three men. It leaned in to face Tsintah with its frighteningly sharp beak and glowing yellow eyes. The bat was massively tall and wide—as massive as a lethal dragon.

"You of all people, Tsintah, know the consequences of disturbing Niyol. Storm Spirit Haseya put me in charge of this cavern, and I cannot let you pass."

The thousands upon thousands of black bats overhead fluttered and squeaked in support of Niyol.

Tsintah whispered over his shoulder at Kokopelli again. "Play!"

Kokopelli hesitated a second, looking at the giant beast, and then closed his eyes and played the high-pitched note.

The bats went crazy above, fluttering and squeaking, and Niyol himself fluttered his wings wide and stamped his feet and leaned in very threateningly close to Tsintah.

"Cease!" Niyol bellowed into the face of Tsintah.

This is exactly what Tsintah wanted, for he touched the temples of Niyol with both glowing green hands and looked deeply into the yellow eyes of the creature. There was a hidden communication between the two, Tsintah and Niyol. Niyol realized that he had unwittingly fallen right into Tsintah's trap, or rather his hands. For Tsintah did not only possess the ability to communicate with animals, but he could, on occasion, use mind control for certain creatures.

Tsintah and Niyol conversed telepathically for several more moments, each looking deeply into the eyes of the other. Then Tsintah simply stated, "I need your help, old friend Niyol."

The giant bat slowly and reluctantly agreed. Niyol then turned and flew up to the lofts of the cavern. Following the lead of their alpha, the other bats inherently knew that they should no further press the issue of the strangers on the floor below.

“Sani, light up the room a bit more,” said Tsintah.

The medicine man then increased the flames on both hands until they noted the hole at the center of the cavern. This was a small hole just like the other one but much darker, and as Kokopelli called into the hole, it was awhile before an echo returned. Tsintah dropped the long and sturdy rope he had been carrying onto the ground. There was also a rock wall behind the deep hole, and in the center of the wall was a small metal hook. On the hook was a tiny golden key.

Tsintah took Spider Mother out of her satchel. He said to her, “Well, spider, time to do your work.”

“My pleasure,” said Spider Mother.

They both smiled back at each other. Spider Mother crawled to the rock wall, climbed up it, and took the golden key off the hook. Then she hurried down the wall, into the deep, deep hole, and out of sight.

Meanwhile, Tsintah and Kokopelli got to work on lowering the rope into the hole. They lowered and lowered and lowered and lowered it down. Then they held tight to it, both men bracing themselves for what might come out of the hole.

At first, there was nothing, just the quiet of the cavern. Even the bats were not fluttering. The medicine man was holding his hands overhead to light the cavern. The two men were bracing hard with the rope. And down below, deep, deep, deep down below ... Spider Mother was moving rapidly with the key toward a single, solitary figure who sat in the dark, chained with fireproof handcuffs and ankle cuffs.

Chapter Twenty-One: The Deepest Pit

Spider Mother neared the figure in the hole but stopped short, hesitating to move farther forward until she knew it was safe. Instinctively, she felt something was off, though she could not quite place it. The single key she held clinked slightly against the damp rock wall in the dark.

"Hello, Spider Mother," began the figure sitting in the dark with a low and gravelly voice. "I've been waiting a long time to hear you. I thank you for coming. I had given up hope of ever getting out of this hole. But sitting here has taught me to listen well—listen to those infernal bats—and I heard when the strangers arrived. I suppose that is Tsintah up top?" asked the man in the dark.

"Yes," said Spider Mother, clearing her throat. "Yes." That was all she could say.

"Ah, Tsintah ... ever a faithful friend. I am certain it was not easy for him to choose to rebel against Haseya. And the two others with him, one plays a flute?"

"That is Kokopelli, a young boy from the cliffs. They have traveled a very long distance to reach you."

"And the other man?"

Spider Mother paused. "That is your son."

The figure sat quietly in the dark and then raised his face so Spider Mother could view him. She could then see in the dark that his eyes were glazed over with white cloudiness. He then said, "Yes, I've been here in the dark for far too long. I've lost my ability to see ... to see my own son. I am blind. Fire Spirit is blind." He said the last phrase with a touch of bitterness.

There was a silence between them as Ahiga the Fire Spirit bowed his head. Spider Mother apologized. Again, more silence. The figure of Ahiga stood up slowly. The fireproof cuffs and chains clinked together.

"Well, come on, Spider Mother. Let's get out of this hole and back to the surface," he said.

Spider Mother moved farther down the wall with the key and then across the dirt ground, dragging the key as she went. She stood in front of Fire Spirit now, and he gently stooped down to lift the key from her. "Thank you," he said as he began to work the key into the locks for his ankles and then his hands. Once he was free of the chains and cuffs, he cast them to the side and carefully rubbed his wrists.

"There is a rope that the others have lowered," explained Spider Mother. "It is to your right."

Fire Spirit took the rope. He knotted the end and climbed onto the knot, balancing his weight carefully against the wall.

"Go up, Spider Mother, and tell the others to pull the rope up. I'll try to climb as well, and we will ascend together."

Spider Mother quickly hurried to the top and told Tsintah and Kokopelli to start pulling the rope. They did as she instructed while Sani kept the flames in his hands. As they pulled the rope farther and farther, Spider Mother explained to the others, "He's been through a lot. He has lost his ability to see, so we will need to guide him out of the cavern and mines."

Tsintah nodded at this new information and added, "I've got a plan to escape the cavern faster. We will use Niyol's help. I intend for us to fly out of the cavern back entrance on the back of Niyol. We will pick up Mai and Sam and head for the cliffs. We need to hurry and get back to the cliffs. There is an impending danger there for the villagers. This is the fastest way."

"Fly on the bat?" said Kokopelli with alarm.

"Yes, I'll show you all what to do. We'll use the rope as reins to secure ourselves to Niyol. Now, keep pulling."

The medicine man wanted to help them pull, but he had to keep the flames going. Meanwhile, overhead, the bats had grown quieter, though they continued to flutter and spread their wings from time to time.

Sani and Tsintah continued to pull with all their might. Ahiga himself appeared to be ascending by climbing the rope as well. Soon, he was pulled to the surface and over the side. There were red scars on his wrists and ankles. His clothes seemed haggard and worn. His hair had grown long and shaggy, and he had a long beard. He lay in the dirt, still holding the rope. Tsintah was first to his side with Spider Mother not far off.

"Ahiga?" he asked.

Fire Spirit turned his face to the sound of Tsintah's voice. He was unable to see Tsintah, but he felt forward with his hands to touch his old friend's shoulders and face. "Tsintah." He smiled.

They hugged each other in the dimly lit cavern. Tsintah touched Fire Spirit's face and checked his wrists and ankles with a look of grave concern. He gently helped Fire Spirit to his feet and away from the hole. Kokopelli and Sani followed eagerly.

"Fire Spirit, I want to introduce you to Kokopelli," began Tsintah.

Fire Spirit nodded and smiled. "Yes, the one with the flute talent. You are a brave young man and clever as well. I thank you."

Tsintah cleared his throat, not knowing at first what to say to introduce Sani. But the medicine man stepped up and said quietly, "Father."

Fire Spirit heard this and turned toward the sound of the voice and smiled with a touch of sadness and happiness all at once and quietly said, "Yes."

Sani lowered one hand, and it was no longer glowing with flame. He reached out to touch his father's arm. Fire Spirit clasped the medicine man's hand in both of his, and then they embraced each other, the fire going out briefly in the dark while they hugged for the first time.

The group then briefly discussed their journey and travels, relaying brief information to Ahiga. They explained the situation at the cliff village and why it was so crucial that they come to rescue Ahiga.

He nodded and said, “Yes, it was time.”

They spoke of the decayers and a possible attack on the village. They spoke of the trials they faced on their journey.

“We’ll need the help of Niyol to return to the cliff village,” said Tsintah.

“No!” said Fire Spirit. “He has held me captive here for too long!”

“That was under the command of Haseya,” began Tsintah. “There is no other way to get back to the village quickly. I fear the decayers may attempt a siege.”

They argued and discussed the matter further, but Tsintah was stubborn and adamant that this should be the plan of action. And so, Niyol was called from the cavern overhead. He stretched and released his grip from the ceiling and then floated effortlessly down to the floor where he landed a few yards away, looking at the travel party with piercing yellow eyes and a sharp, dangerous beak.

Tsintah walked over to Niyol. After a brief exchange and a meeting of the minds between the two of them, Niyol lowered his body to the ground so the others could climb aboard. He was a giant beast of a bat, and there was plenty of room for the others to settle onto his back and away from his massive wings. Tsintah secured the long rope in front of Niyol and around his neck. He told the others to hold on tightly to each other and the rope. Tsintah and Niyol had already discussed the secret back entrance to the cavern. So Tsintah pointed in the direction of the route and said, “Fly.”

Niyol took a second or two to open and expand his tremendous wings. Then he lifted off the ground, hovering momentarily with the travel party on his back. He then flew higher, up toward the cavern ceiling. He flew north into the back of the cavern and through a large slit in the rock walls. Kokopelli and Sani held tightly to the rope and to the back of the bat as he carried them through a rocky tunnel and around stalactites and stalagmites. They flew faster and faster. The bat deftly dodged to the left and right and at one point turned slightly up and sideways to pass a large obstruction in the way. Everyone held tightly to the ropes and to the bat and to their own breath. None of the travel party except Tsintah had ever flown before. The excitement and adrenaline were coursing through their veins, and their hearts were hammering in their chests. Ahiga, although he could not see, was also clinging tightly to the ropes and to the side of Tsintah, who fearlessly held the reins to the bat. He sat in the front, helping to guide Niyol and checking to make certain everyone was staying on and secure to the rope. They flew and flew through the dark tunnel with Niyol's yellow eyes showing the way out. Once they crossed the final rock crevice and were out in the open, the strong Colorado wind blasted against them. Kokopelli and Sani struggled with their ropes. The medicine man reached to pull Kokopelli back up and into the ropes and onto the center of the bat.

"Look out!" he called. "Stay with me! Hold on!"

Kokopelli grasped for Sani's help, and together they huddled on the bat as it glided effortlessly into the still night. They had come out into a valley region near the back of the mountain. The bat began to ascend carefully on the winds and circle back to the front of the mountain as directed by Tsintah so they could pick up Mai, Sam, and Kai. The full moon shone brightly on the quiet group as they flew over tall forests of coniferous trees. The wind was cold on the travel party, and they huddled together, clinging to the ropes. Up they glided on the winds and around the mountain until they once again saw the three cabins of the abandoned mine company. The bat descended as ordered by Tsintah until it alighted on the ground. Tsintah then left the others with the bat. He went to the third cabin where Mai, Sam, and Kai were waiting. He helped them gather their things. Then each one stepped onto the bat's back and settled in amid the ropes and huddled closely together with the others.

Kokopelli was relieved to see Mai and Kai again. He took his satchel and opened it a little to peer inside and see Izou waiting for him. But he closed the satchel before Izou could get out because he did not want the lizard loose. When everyone was secured and ready, Niyol ascended again. As before, he hovered in the air with his enormous wings flapping in the breeze. Then, ever so carefully, he moved higher and higher into the clouds above the mountains and headed toward the cliff village.

Ahiga was huddled near Tsintah, and they spoke to each other softly so the others could not hear.

"This will alert Haseya," said Fire Spirit. "She will know we are coming if we enter the sky with Niyol. This is storm territory. She cannot help but know we are coming. She will do something."

"I know this," said Tsintah matter-of-factly and resolute in his answer. He looked down onto the land so far below them now. "This is her realm. We cannot hide from her any longer, but I know Haseya well. She already knows what we have been up to. There was a rain storm just prior to our arrival here. I do believe the timing of that rain storm was no accident. I fear she has been studying us for a while now. For whatever reason, she has chosen not to interfere, and so I took a chance tonight in using Niyol. We've got to get back to the cliff village. It was a gamble I was willing to take."

Tsintah looked ahead into the clouds as the rest of the travel party huddled closely together in the cold winds of the night sky. "But, Ahiga, you are right. She will come. I don't know when. I don't know how. But it will happen. She knows and she will come for us." Tsintah watched the clouds around them very carefully that night.

Chapter Twenty-Two: Battle of the Beasts

Under the cover of darkness in the early hours before dawn, the evil shape-shifter horde began their approach on the cliff village. They had planned a coordinated attack on the unsuspecting villagers and intended to capture every inhabitant, man, woman, and child. They needed human vessels to become more powerful skinwalkers. The Hyaenodon led the way, though he had decided to shift into his humanoid creature form. He ran swiftly across the land with his spear and was followed by the council of twenty in various forms, as well as the three hundred or more adults of the decayer community. Amid the horde, there were shape-shifters as coyotes, dire wolves, cougars, black dogs, black bears, and others who chose to follow Hashkeh Naabah's lead and keep their humanoid form. They stealthily poured across the land, galloping on all fours or running on two. Flying overhead were the monstrous predatory black birds called teratornis, which kept equal pace to the horde. The minion shape-shifters moved silently, though rapidly, across the ground using their night vision to see across the tar pits outside the decayer domain. They climbed Rattlesnake Ridge and descended en masse through the thick forests and plains and onto the sparse canyon lands just west of the lush Hanahu Valley below the cliffs ahead. The villagers of the cliffs had no warning of the looming danger.

At daybreak, the horde entered the canyon lands and proceeded to cross. They entered the center fields of the canyons. Behind them stood the rocky and treacherous pathway up hill to Rattlesnake Ridge. To their right was the massive expanse of the canyon lands leading south. To their left was more canyon lands leading north. To their front, to the east facing them was the last solitary hill before entrance into the Hanahu Valley. And standing on the crest of the hill was a tiny figure, an almost doll-like creature.

Hashkeh Naabah halted the encroaching horde, and together, they spread out along the canyon lands like a massive wall of predatory beasts and humanoid creatures. The only thing stopping them was the lone figure standing on the hill. Hashkeh Naabah eyed the doll with suspicion and looked around them in all directions. From the horde came the cackles of the witch shape-shifters, as well as low, guttural growling, the gnashing of teeth, and the pawing of the dirt.

At the top of the hill, Yanaha stood watching the predators approaching rapidly. When he was certain they had stopped to survey him with menacing curiosity, Yanaha took the horn in his hands and blew loudly. The sound of the horn echoed through the canyon, and for a moment, there was nothing to be heard or felt but the canyon breeze. Then a loud rumbling came from behind the hill, a thunderous rumbling. First, the birds appeared. Bald eagles, each with a kachina doll rider, rose into the skies overhead and darted forward across the canyon expanse to attack the black teratornis birds. One solo bald eagle swooped down effortlessly to catch Yanaha, who climbed onto the bird's back. These were the nature spirit allies. The bald eagles, approximately fifty of them, flew straight at the teratornis birds, and the air battle became vicious with the tearing of wings and the use of talons and beaks by each side. The rumbling past the hill became louder too, and soon a giant herd of buffalo nature spirit allies crested the top. They stampeded down the other side of the hill in unison and into the center of the shape-shifter horde. From the left and right of the buffalo herd also descended into the canyon lands a cavalry of mustang horses and a barrage of grizzly bears galloping into the horde flanks. The nature spirit allies were attacking the shape-shifter horde to defend the cliff village.

The battle was fierce and intense as the nature spirits summoned by Yanaha went on the attack against the shape-shifter predatory horde. But the coyotes and dire wolves, the black dogs and cougars answered back with fangs bared. The horses kicked and attacked, but the wolves were pulling them down one by one. The grizzlies went head to head with the black bears and humanoid creatures. They fought viciously in hand-to-hand combat. Hashkeh Naabah at the front used his claws and knives, as well as his spear, to defeat animal after animal.

The battle continued among the beasts, and there were shrieks and screams, roars and neighing coming from all sides in the thick of the battle. But the predatory beasts were more cunning and ruthless and were beginning to get the upper hand on the nature spirit allies. One by one, the nature spirits were getting pulled down. In the air, the kachina dolls fought bravely with bows and arrows against the threatening teratornis birds. They darted in and out and looped high and low into the sky, evading and attacking. Yanaha had three teratornis birds on his tail when he noticed far off to his left in the east something descending onto the Hanahu Valley from the clouds.

Tsintah and Niyol with the travel party had arrived at the cliffs. They were alerted to the sounds coming from the west. After inspecting the cliff village from a distance to make certain everyone there was all right, they flew straight onward to the canyon lands where they could see the massive battle of the beasts. The giant bat lowered quickly to the ground at the east base of the hill.

Tsintah stayed on Niyol and told the others, "Get off the bat! Stay here at the east base of the hill. Sani, take Ahiga to the crest of the hill now. I'm going to the other side of the canyon with Niyol. I will order the nature spirit retreat. Ahiga, get to the top of the hill. You will know what to do when the time comes."

The others hurried off the giant bat, and Tsintah and Niyol lifted into the air again. They flew far to the north and then over to the west to the far-reaching side of the canyon beyond the horde. Meanwhile, the medicine man helped his blind father, Fire Spirit, to the top of the hill. Then Tsintah directed Niyol to fly low and fast over the beasts below. As they flew, spears were launched into the air at the giant bat, which deftly dodged them.

Tsintah called out over and over again, "Retreat! Retreat, nature spirits! Run over the hill to the east. Retreat! To the east hill! Retreat!"

Slowly, the beasts began to disentangle themselves from each other, and the nature spirits that were left retreated as best they could back over the hill past Sani and Ahiga as they crested the hilltop. Fire Spirit was listening and holding on to the arms of the medicine man. Hashkeh Naabah saw them on the hill and began to move forward to advance upon them. Suddenly, the ground beneath him tremored and shifted. Hashkeh Naabah growled and turned quickly to look back behind the horde. Niyol was now off to the north and west side of the canyon land. Tsintah was off the bat and was kneeling down in his green hooded cloak as he touched the earth with both hands, which were glowing bright green. The earth shook and tremored violently again, and the ground under Tsintah's outstretched hands began to rip apart. The impending earthquake brought by his hands drew a sharp and jagged barrier across the canyon land expanse to the west, preventing the horde's escape back across Rattlesnake Ridge. The earth ripped apart deeply, and some of the last horde members started to fall into the crevices brought about by the violent earthquake.

When Fire Spirit felt the first tremors of the earth, he pushed his son away from him and down the hill to the east and away from the horde. He could not see, so he pushed him hard enough to drive Sani far away. Then, Fire Spirit turned swiftly and faced the canyon lands. He could not be certain that all the nature spirits had managed to retreat over the hill, but he had to entrap the shape-shifters. He raised his arms wide, stretching them out to either side, and there was a massive explosion of fire from the ground. It forced everyone back on either side in a rapid blast of heat. As the horde fell back, more and more stragglers on the other side fell into the earth's crevices. An all-consuming gigantic firewall of flames rose high around Ahiga and into the sky as far reaching to the north and south as possible and far up high to block the teratornis birds from overcoming it. The fire blazed massively hot and terrible, and in the center of it stood Fire Spirit, ablaze himself with outstretched arms and yet vulnerable to attack. From the other side of the hill, the remaining nature spirits and eagles with kachina dolls fell back from the fire. Mai with Kai, Sam, and Kokopelli fell back as well, covering their faces with their arms. Only the medicine man ventured closer to the fire, knowing full well that his father could be exposed to Hashkeh Naabah's advance. But he could not get through the fire and watched helplessly with grave concern.

"No!" he called.

Tsintah watched the massive firewall from the northwest side. He stood up slowly and watched what was happening with the horde of predators with great trepidation. They were in a panic from being encircled. They could not retreat west nor advance east. There was great howling and shrieks and cries and gnashing of teeth. Meanwhile, Hashkeh Naabah grabbed with great vengeance a nearby spear in a horse. He watched Fire Spirit with exceeding anger and seething hatred. He began to move up the hill to the firewall with spear in hand. When he was eight feet from the blind spirit, he slowly reached back his spear arm to deliver a brutal blow.

"No!" cried Tsintah.

The winds picked up. Tsintah looked to the sky and whispered, "Storm Spirit."

To the north, something flashed brilliantly from the sky and hurled itself violently toward the earth. It moved with incredible speed and slammed into the ground, causing the earth to crack and break open where it landed. It was a woman who landed hard with her fist slammed into the dirt and bent over into a half-kneeling stance. Meanwhile, there came a strange sound from above the horde, and the predators, including Hashkeh Naabah, looked to the sky above them. The sky made a hollow sound like wind in a giant tunnel, and the teratornis birds began to flutter and caw in panicked unison. They flapped their wings and attempted to flee into the sky away from the louder and louder sucking noise overhead, the hollow wind tunnel noise that grew and grew. The skies became quickly dark, and the clouds overhead churned like a monstrous cyclone. Overhead, the beasts could now see a dark, treacherous tornado spout more than a mile wide covering the skies and threatening to slam down. The woman to the north stood up and brushed the dirt off herself. She faced Hashkeh Naabah who had stopped his throw in midstride to stare at the massive sky hole overhead.

"I'm late to the party," she began, and she strolled purposely forward with hands fisted. She spoke to the decayers now. "You thought you'd start a little storm, but I've brought one better. I'm a force of nature, and you're gonna wish you never crossed that bridge nor crossed me." She then promptly brought her hands together.

The rolling and rumbling winds of the tornado were then unleashed and crashed down on the screaming horde. It was a tremendous and dark, terrifying tornado that rapidly sucked all of them, including Hashkeh Naabah, into the sky. The sound was deafening. The terror overpowering. And then just as quickly as it had arrived, it suddenly lifted away.

Chapter Twenty-Three: Earth, Wind, and Fire

In the wake of the deadly tornado, the only ones left remaining in the canyon were the three gods, Earth, Wind, and Fire. Haseya motioned to Tsintah to meet her in the central plain amid the destruction and devastation. Ahiga, sensing the tornado had left and the horde was gone, slowly lowered the fire wall and remained in place at the top of the hill. First, Haseya and Tsintah spoke.

"You disobeyed me," Haseya said sternly, her hands balled into fists at her sides. But then her face softened. "You broke the elemental laws. Yet, perhaps it was time for this all to be over. You have always known what was best, Tsintah."

At the leniency exhibited, Tsintah bowed his head. He did not speak yet.

"It will be difficult to speak to Ahiga about the past," she said, nodding toward the hill. "You should speak first."

Again, Tsintah nodded.

The two gods turned and walked side by side to the hill. Tsintah was still cloaked as before but with a lowered hood. Haseya was dressed in a blue and tassled knee-length dress. She wore sandals tied to her calves. Her hair was long and flowing in beautiful shades of brown. Her eyes were also brown. She walked casually toward Ahiga until they were within a short distance.

Tsintah spoke first. "Ahiga, your time of punishment is over, according to Haseya. She is with me now and wants to speak with you."

"I know you are with Tsintah, Haseya." There was resentment and measurable anger in Ahiga's tone.

"I offer you my healing powers, Ahiga. You know I have the

ability to return your sight. I want our fight to be over, and I want you to return to the spirit realm with Tsintah and me. I know you are angry at me but you broke the elemental laws."

Fire Spirit listened but did not speak yet.

"I am ... sorry for enforcing the Elemental Code and," Haseya said with sincerity, "for my jealousy and anger over your relationship with the mortal woman. You disobeyed before. You broke the rules but I understand that you were protecting the ones whom you love." She said this while looking at Sani. "However, you broke the code of the elements and for that, it was necessary for you to be punished."

"Sorry does not bring back what I have lost," he said with frustration.

Storm Spirit stepped forward until she was within reach of Fire Spirit. He looked ahead, feeling her presence but not truly seeing her. She raised her hands to his eyes, and white orbs of light gathered at her fingertips. She closed her eyes, and when she opened them again, she removed her hands so that Ahiga could see again.

He blinked several times over.

She stepped back and turned to walk away. "I offer you the chance to return home. I do not offer this lightly. I will give you some time with your son and the villagers. In a fortnight, Tsintah and Tahoma and I will return to take you home if you are ready. Your son, Sani, as well as his friends have done much to rescue you and save their cliff village. To be honest, I have been watching since nearly the beginning of this journey. I could have intervened at any moment to stop what happened, but I too wanted an end to this dispute and the enforcement of the elemental code. Your son, Sani, is very wise and brave, and his travel companions have shown much courage in the face of adversity. You have much to make you proud."

And with that, both Tsintah and Haseya walked out onto the canyon lands and then shot high into the sky, launching from the ground in one great bolt of light. They disappeared into the heavens.

In the days to come, Fire Spirit and the medicine man worked side by side to restore the damage done by the battle and to rebuild and repair the community as needed. They enjoyed the time bonding together after such a long absence from each other.

Ahiga made an offer to Sani to go to the spirit realm with him where he would live as a demigod, but the medicine man shook his head sadly. He chose to stay with crow and the kachina dolls and to continue to look over the cliff village community. Kokopelli and Mai later became apprentices of the medicine man. Kai was happily reunited with his mother and father. His mother and father cried great tears of joy at Kai's return and they hugged their two other children fiercely.

On the final night before Fire Spirit's departure, the cliff villagers threw a celebration in his honor. At the party, Kokopelli played the flute for the entertainment for all, particularly for the love and joy of his family—his father, his mother, his sister Mai, and baby Kai. Later that night, Ahiga slipped away from the village and walked out onto the cliffs by himself. Soon, he was met by Tsintah, Tahoma, and Haseya. He took one fond look at the fire lights of the little cliff village and at the shadows of the dancing villagers. He looked once more with deep love for his son, Sani. He listened to the sound of the joyful flute in the distance. Then he nodded to the others. Together, the elementals ascended rapidly to the sky in a bolt of light.

Balance and order among the elements had finally been restored. And this fourth world, the world of his beloved son and friends, this world would continue on.

www.ingramcontent.com/pod-product-compliance
Lightning Source LLC
Chambersburg PA
CBHW030146010826
48973CB00002B/747

* 9 7 8 1 9 6 3 7 1 8 4 7 8 *